Nirvana

A Forbidden Romance Series Novel

by Shevaun DeLucia

Gary—
Congrats on the win!.
Enjoy :)

Shevaun DeLucia

Words Written, LLC
Rochester, New York

Words Written, LLC
New York
www.shevaundelucia.com

Book Layout by Alchemy and Words
http://www.alchemyandwords.com/

Cover Art by Sommer Stein
http://www.perfectpearcreative.com/

Nirvana/ Shevaun DeLucia
ISBN 978-0-9863951-5-4

Dedication

To Kiki for pushing me to sit my butt down and write.

nirvana

noun, often capitalized nir·va·na \nir-ˈvä-nə, (ˌ)nər-\
: a state or place of great happiness and peace

CHAPTER ONE

Junior

"Fuck!" I pick up the red pumps I just tripped over and throw them across the room. I seriously almost just broke my dang neck. This chick is out of control! I mean, who leaves their crap in the middle of the walkway? Where the hell was she raised, a barn?

I slam my briefcase on the kitchen counter. I hear bare footsteps slapping against the wood floor behind me.

"What the fuck are you all huffy about? Did somebody piss in your Wheaties?" Kinsey antagonizes, knowing she'll get a reaction.

She walks by me to get a glass out of the cupboard. She's wearing a white, very thin tank with some extremely tiny shorts. When she reaches up, the bottom of her booty cheeks pop out slightly. Damn her. I immediately look away. I refuse to indulge in her skimpy, alluring attire.

"Can you please place your shoes on the mat where

they belong so I don't trip over them again?" I growl, quickly turning and stomping to my room. I hear her curse behind my back.

Man, she gets my blood boiling like no other girl. She's just impossible. She makes me want to rip my hair out of my head. I've never met anyone so aggravating in my entire life. Only a couple more months and the lease is up, and then I can get my own place. I only agreed to be her roommate to help Max out when she became pregnant and bought a house with my brother, Kyle. At the time, I needed a place to stay other than my parents', because the place I was renting was going up for sale. This was a quick fix for the both of us, but I'm ready to get the hell out of here.

It's been a long day. I need a hot shower to ease my stiff muscles from the tension. Working as a literary agent for my father has its ups and downs, but today was a rough one. When he gets in his psychotic freak-out moods, it's just better to stay away. Unfortunately, sometimes it's impossible, especially when it's regarding one of my clients.

I began working for my family at the Saunders Literary Agency straight out of high school. My father mentored me for years and made me take night classes at the community college to earn my degree before moving me up as an agent. I never shared that with my brother. I didn't attend college out of state like Kyle did, and in some ways I envy him for it. I wish I would have allowed myself that experience.

I completely robbed myself of girls, booze, and frat parties in exchange for the business world of suits and ties —but who am I fooling? I would have never fit in, regardless. It's just not my thing.

I have a lot of built-up resentment toward Kyle, stemming from our childhood years. Eventually that resentment turned into something much bigger and deeper. Yes, I actually despise my little brother now. Maybe I'm a dick for feeling this way, but it's just how I feel. Simple as that.

I hop out of the shower and hear my phone ringing.

I see Jeff's number across my phone screen. "Hello?"

"What's up, man? Kyle and I are gonna check out this new bar, The Tavern. You wanna come? Max is letting him off of the chain for a while," Jeff jokes.

I take the phone away from my ear to look at the time. It's now quarter to six, and I still have some energy left that I need to exhaust. This would sound perfect if my brother was out of the equation, but it beats sitting in this house with Kinsey, so I'm game.

"Yeah, man. I'm down. Just tell Kyle to keep his trap shut, and we'll be fine," I warn.

I hear Jeff snicker on the other end before hanging up.

I get dressed into my favorite faded jeans and black T, and top it off with some Jimmy Choo cologne. I don't envision myself meeting my future wife at the bar. I'm not like the rest of these dudes—wham, bam, thank you ma'am is not my style. I would rather do the dinner-and-date sort of thing where I take the time to get to know someone— laugh and share stories over candlelight. This idea seems so foreign to women these days. I know I need to broaden my horizons and start venturing out to places other than the bar scene. If I don't make the effort and switch up my routine, I'm going to be stuck by myself—miserable and alone.

Music begins to blare from the living room. Great. Taylor Swift. Isn't this crap for teenagers? I feel like I'm living with one most of the time anyways, so I guess this fits. I head out of my room and into the kitchen. Kinsey is dancing around like she is having convulsions while cooking on the stove. Whatever she's making smells mighty good, though.

"Hey tight ass. You hungry?" she yells.

Does this chick own any sweats? She's still half naked! My southern region stirs just a bit. Damn it. I roll my eyes and try to think of my grandma. "No, I'm going out," I growl before heading to the door. A wave of guilt washes over me for being so abrupt with her. She didn't deserve that. I turn toward her. "Thank you, though."

She gives me a bright smile. "Don't be too late, dear!" she adds. Okay, maybe I should have stuck with the crass me. I don't even turn to acknowledge her nonsense. I give praise to whoever ends up with her and can put up with her insane, aggravating self.

I step out into the crisp air. Fall is in full effect, with winter on the cusp. I zip my jacket up to my neck and head out to my car.

I pull up to this new bar, The Tavern, and it looks promising. Cars are filling up the parking lot, and it's only Monday. It's only ten minutes from my apartment, which is a major bonus. Let's just hope Beth's crew hasn't found out about this location. I can't stand a woman desperate and always on the prowl for the next victim. You would think a woman would get tired of constantly being used as a cum dumpster.

I shut the car off and head to the front door. I get excited as I walk up, because I see my man, Jonas, bouncing at the door.

I slap his hand up, bringing him in for a brief hug. "Hey, man! What's up? How've you been? I haven't seen you in forever!" I say ecstatically.

"Man, tell me about it! I actually just moved back from Arizona. My dad's sick, so he needed someone to help take care of him," he responds.

I shake my head. "Damn, sorry to hear that. How

was it in the desert?"

A guy comes up the stairs behind me. I scoot over and wait for Jonas to finish ID-ing him.

"It's fucking *amazing* out there! It's a whole different world. A different type of living," he responds. I have to admit, Arizona has never been one of my bucket-list destinations, but he's making it seem pretty damn intriguing.

"Sounds nice, man. You got family out there?" I ask.

Jonas grabs a cigarette from his jacket pocket and lights it up, immediately exhaling the smoke. "Yeah, my mom moved out there. I headed out there after we graduated," he says. He pulls out his phone from his back pocket and shows me a picture of a little girl. "This is my daughter, Sabrina. She just turned three." He beams with pride.

"That's awesome, man. She's beautiful. Wow, I can't believe you had a kid!" Jonas was quarterback of the football team, a crazy partier who I was sure didn't have it in him to settle down, let alone have a kid! He should have made it to the NFL, but he had a major injury that cost him his career senior year.

"Yeah, tell me about it. It was sort of a one-night hookup that went completely wrong, but I wouldn't trade Sabrina for the world. Her mom and I get along pretty well, considering," he finishes with a shrug.

"It was great seeing you, man," I tell him. I type my number into his phone quickly and then give him a quick side-hug. "Let's meet up soon!"

"For sure, Junior. Don't get too crazy in there!" he jokes.

I head inside and see Jeff and Kyle at the bar with beers already in hand.

"Damn, about time, bro!" Jeff yells. I shake my head. Loud mouth. "Did you run into Jonas at the door?"

The bartender asks me what I would like. "Um, I'll take a Heineken." She grabs the bottle from the fridge below and pops the top before placing it in front of me. "Thank you."

"I was just talking to him outside. It's like talking to a ghost. I can't believe it's been this long," I respond.

"Dude, you ain't lying. All the drunken nights came flying back to me real quick!" Jeff says, laughing.

Kyle speaks up. "Yeah, I played wingman for most of those crazy nights! Now look at us! I have a daughter, and you're finally tied down. Who would have ever thought?"

I take a sip of my beer. "Yeah, and I'm living with a loud-mouth woman who still acts like a spoiled teenager!"

Jeff laughs loudly, and Kyle just shakes his head with a smirk. "Dude, who cares if she's a wacko mess; she's hot as fuck! Why haven't you even attempted to tap that ass?" Jeff questions.

Ahh, the old Jeff peeks through the rainbows and sunshine. "Not all men like to hit it and quit it like you two used to. Besides, didn't anyone tell you not to shit where you lie? That's the golden rule. Anyways, she may be hot, but she's not my type whatsoever!"

Kyle rolls his eyes, which makes me want to lay his ass out. "What, Kyle? Is there something you want to say?" I growl.

"Yeah, there is, actually. Maybe if you stop

following all these rules you're giving yourself, you might actually enjoy life and find yourself a girl to settle down with," Kyle responds.

I shake my head. "Now you know all about life, because you've found Max? Let me tell you something *little* brother—not everyone is so lucky. Some people have to actually work hard at life. Some people actually have morals and values they live by. I'm not giving them up just for a little fun. So do me a favor, next time you have something to say, keep your damn mouth shut," I tell him, taking a long pull from my beer.

"Hey, you're the one that asked what was on my mind. Next time, don't ask, and I won't say shit!" Kyle spits out.

Jeff steps in as usual. "Alright, alright. Come on, both of you just chill out," Jeff says. He yells to the bartender for a round of shots. "Let's just relax and enjoy the night. Look around us—we're free of Beth's crew! We can actually drink in peace."

I nod my head. "This is a cool little spot, but it's only a matter of time before everyone gets wind of it."

The bartender sets out three shot glasses and pours the chilled Patrón evenly. Jeff pays and slides our shots to us. We hold them up while Jeff makes a quick dedication, "To brotherhood and friendship! Salute!"

"Salute!" Kyle and I follow. We throw back the burning liquid.

"So, how's my awesome goddaughter?" Jeff asks Kyle.

His face lights up with the thought of her. Another thing I envy. I can picture myself settled down with a wife and kid. I never really entertained this thought before, but I also never thought my little brother would be the first. Recently, I feel the desire evolving.

"Man, she's fucking amazing! She just started sitting up on her own, and Max has been going crazy, baby-proofing the whole house. She feels like Penelope is going to crawl early. She's so smart that Max is afraid she will figure out how to open the cupboards with the latches on them, so we switched to the magnetic locks. I know she's totally going overboard, but I think we're now fully prepared for that moment to come," Kyle explains like a proud father. Jealously erupts, and I have to swallow it back down.

We all laugh for once. "That's my girl! Elise and I are gonna stop by and visit with her sometime this week. I miss that little angel. It's crazy how one little girl can have me wrapped around her finger so tightly. I don't want to even think about her dating," Jeff huffs. Kyle and I both exhale loudly. Neither of us want to think of that moment yet.

"All I can picture is that damn *Bad Boys* scene—" Kyle begins to say.

"Oh hell yeah! We're gonna be the uncles from hell!" Jeff yells out with a laugh. I have to agree with him on this one.

I jump in. "She'll never want to date again after we're done! Kyle, let me ask you something—" I begin, trying my hardest not to sound too abrasive or rude.

"Shoot."

"What will you do if she ends up with someone like you two when she gets older? Are you ready to own your mistakes and teach her how to protect herself from guys like you?" I ask. He may see this as me antagonizing him, but I truly want to know the answer. I want to know if he's thought this far into the future and if he regrets his lack of respect for the girls in his past.

Kyle pauses and thinks for a moment. "Your're damn right I am going to! I'm going to treat her like a princess so she knows no less. I'm going to teach her how to respect herself and protect herself from scums like us. I'm going to show her unconditional and endless love so she doesn't have the need to find it in some cold, heartless punk. I'm going to do whatever it takes to make sure my baby only has the best in life. She's the love of my life, and I hope to be the love in hers until she finds the one who can fill my spot. Does that sound insane?" he wonders.

I have to admit my heart tightens just a bit. I think I may have just gained an ounce of respect for my brother. Who would have thought?

Jeff raises his beer, and I follow. We all clink them together and take a long pull. My beer is empty, and I signal the bartender for another round.

"So Jeff, how is the monogamous life treating you?

Elise seemed pretty happy today when I walked by her," I ask.

He looks pretty proud of himself at the moment. "Oh you know, I had to get my lady some flowers delivered. It's her third year working at the agency. I've realized that it's the little things that matter. She's not too big on over-the-top, extravagant things. I totally love that about her," he explains, glowing. I don't know how much more of this rainbows-and-sunshine shit I can take. "Actually, she wants to have everyone over Friday night for some pizza and beer. You guys game?"

Shit! Kyle and Kinsey in the same house? I guess I can play nice as long as they both stay on opposite sides of the room.

"Yeah, man. I'm down. Let me know if there's something you need me to bring," I say. Kyle says he will be there as well. I guess it will give me some extra quality time with my niece, who I don't see nearly as much as I should.

We have another round of shots and beers, then call it a night. Duty calls in the morning for the three of us, and these guys have women who will be calling their phones very shortly if they're not home.

    I pull into the parking garage. To others, it may be eerily quiet, but to me, it's sort of soothing. I'm so used to being by myself that the silence doesn't phase me that much. Ever since I moved in with Kinsey, I barely get those moments alone, unless she's out on a date or with the girls. Sometimes I stay late at work just to purposely avoid her. She drives me absolutely insane.

    She stirs something inside of me. A wide range of emotions I never knew existed. I'm not quite sure what this means, but it's pretty frustrating, just as she is. The worst part is that she knows this, and she likes to push all my buttons. It's like she *enjoys* seeing my reactions, and it pisses me the fuck off, quite frankly!

    I head up the elevator. I reach the apartment door, and it's quiet. Hmm. I place my ear against the door before putting my key in the doorknob. I just want to make sure the coast is clear before I enter her lair.

The lights are all dim except for the kitchen. Before I have the chance to lock the door behind me, I see Kinsey sitting at the kitchen counter, surrounded by paperwork and a glass of red wine. *Shit!* I was hoping she would have turned in already. I knew it was too good to be true. I just freaking knew it! I celebrated too early.

"Hey sunshine, I see you made it home before curfew," she teases. I roll my eyes. Does this girl ever stop?

"More like Kyle and Jeff's curfew," I add.

She laughs. "I can only imagine. Max was probably waiting at the door for Kyle. She said Penelope is teething, and the poor girl won't go down for bed. I feel sorry for Mr. Kyle tonight—no nooky for him!" she says with an evil smirk. I think I just saw horns ascending from her head.

"Chill woman, before I have to cast you back down to hell," I say to her sarcastically.

She sticks out her tongue and then pours some more wine. At least the woman has good taste; Nosotros is the best of the best. My father schooled me well. She must see me eyeing the bottle. "Go get a glass if you want some.

I'll share, sweet cheeks."

I shake my head. "No, I'm good. What's with the pet names, though? Do you enjoy getting a reaction from it?" I question, leaning my backside against the countertop and crossing my arms over my chest. I'm dying to hear this answer.

She pretends to be offended. "Moi?" she asks, smirking. She then takes a sip of her wine. "Aww, come on! Does it really bother you that much?"

I'm kinda feeling like a jackass at the moment; like I've just overreacted a tad. "It's annoying," I tell her bluntly.

She takes another sip of wine while considering my answer. If she keeps sucking that down, I may have to carry her to her bed. "Okay, let's make a deal—sit down and have a glass of wine with me, and I will bite my tongue for the rest of the night. How's that sound?"

"How about I just call it a night, and we both win without the extra dramatics?" I suggest.

She pouts, pushing her bottom lip out. I really want to walk over to her and bite it. *Shit!* Where the fuck did that just come from? I look away quickly to gather my thoughts.

"You're no fun! We're roomies for god's sake! Let loose for just one minute. It isn't going to kill you to have a drink with me. We've been living together for nearly a year now, and I barely even know you."

She's completely right. I try hard to avoid her at all costs. She just isn't my cup of tea, but I'm buzzed and I guess it wouldn't hurt to have a drink with her. Sober, I would never agree to this. If anything, it will shut her up. I turn to grab a glass from the cupboard and place it in front of her.

She smirks with satisfaction. I can't help but chuckle. She has a great smile. "See, that wasn't so hard, now was it?" she says while pouring the wine. "So, I'm going over the proposal for the Jefferson memoir for Max. Can I run some things by you?"

Now she has me intrigued. "Yeah, OK. Go for it." What's a little work while I'm buzzed?

She flips through the pages in front of her, and we begin.

After going over the whole proposal with her, I finally call it a night. I have to admit, I actually enjoyed this one-on-one time with her. She's still a smart ass, but she held her tongue with the funky name-calling like she promised.

I remove all my clothes and put on my sweats. I'm a commando sorta guy. I would sleep naked if I didn't have a female roommate. I've been known to sleepwalk once in a blue moon, and I know I would never live that down with Kinsey.

I crack a smile thinking of her out-of-control, crazy self, but I quickly recover by remembering how obnoxious she can be. It's clear I'm buzzed and overtired. On that note, I shut off the light and slam my eyes shut, letting the dark consume me.

CHAPTER TWO

Kinsey

I watch Junior head off to bed, and I have to admit that the girls are right—his backside is definitely worth a look. I almost cringe thinking this, but hey, I'm still a hot-blooded, single girl, right? So why not? He was actually enjoyable tonight—humanlike, unlike the last couple of months I've shared with him. I think this is the first time we've had a normal adult conversation. Usually it's a bunch of huffing and eyerolling on both our parts.

My phone dings, signaling a text. My brows furrow. I don't recognize the number. I open the message and after reading it, it dawns on me that this is from Jax, the guy I met last week at Starbucks while getting my Macchiato before work.

"Hey Kinsey, it's Jax from Starbucks. You free tomorrow night for a drink?" he texts.

This is a nice surprise. Took him long enough though. "I am. Where do you have in mind?" I text back.

"There's a new bar, The Tavern, that just opened

up. It's over on West Street. How does 6pm sound?" he replies.

"I'll see you there! "

It's been a couple of weeks since I went out on a date. The last one didn't turn out so good. I ended up throwing a drink on some guy's narcissistic ass and told him to suck it! He got the hint real quick. He was a douche, but the look on his face was priceless! Let's just hope this date doesn't follow suit. I may not be able to recover this time around. I almost lost hope for all mankind.

I got up early this morning in an optimistic mood and decided to curl my hair today. Why not? I have a date tonight, so I might as well put a little effort in my appearance. If the date turns out disastrous, then at least my hair will have looked good for work.

I put my earrings on and head out of my room, slamming smack dab into Junior's steel body. Damn it. I glance up at him momentarily, palms against his swollen chest, and we lock eyes for just a split second. Weird things happen. For once, I am completely speechless. How is this possible? I am *never* speechless. Then he speaks, and I gain all sense and my smart wit back.

"Damn, woman! Watch where you're going!" he snaps.

Oh hell no! I quickly remove my hands and whip myself around, hair all up in his face. Screw him! This is how he wants to start the day off after having a nice night last night? "Don't get your tighty whities in a bunch with me because you didn't get laid last night. Get that stick out of your ass, and you just might get some pussy," I growl.

I look back with a bitchy smirk, and I see him cringe from my comment. Good, that's what he gets.

"Why do you always have to be so darn vulgar? It's freaking eight in the morning for Chrissake!" he spits out, following me into the kitchen.

I always put the coffee on the timer setting so it brews enough for the both of us. He should be thanking me instead of biting my head off. Hmmm. Tomorrow I will make enough for just me. That ought to teach him a lesson.

We both hostilely make our coffee. I even left a

mug out for him. Asshole. "Then don't piss me off! We had a nice time last night, and now all I have left in my mouth is the taste of your bitterness. Way to go, jackass!" I finish like a crazy woman and walk to the front door, slamming it behind me. Okay, maybe a little dramatic, but geez, he didn't have to flip the script with me before I even had my coffee.

I get to work and Max already has ten-plus sticky notes attached to my door for me. I can see it's going to be one of *those* days. I downed my coffee on the way here. I think I may need something a little stronger for lunchtime though.

"Hey, Kins!" Max comes in and flops herself down on the chair in front of me. I shake my head and chuckle.

"What's up, chick? How did last night go?"

Max blows out a huge breath. "Well, Kyle thought he was getting lucky last night, until he walked in and saw Penelope on my lap and me with a huge glass of wine!" she explains.

I laugh. I can only imagine his face turned from seductive sexual deviant to sad little schoolboy. "Aww! Poor Kyle. This no-sex-every-day thing must be rough on him," I state.

I pull up my email. The messages pile up right in front of my eyes. "How is it I come in early and even leave late, and I *still* have a million emails to answer too?" I gripe, slamming my head into my hands.

Max just laughs. I look up and give her the stank face. "You should see my emails," Max says, shaking her head. "I got here an hour and a half ago, and I still haven't caught up! I handed Kyle the baby last night and took my ass to bed! She exhausted me. This teething thing is so hard. I hate that my baby is in pain. And honestly, I could use a nice dose of sex right about now. I've been too tired to act on it though. Kyle is so great about it. He's so patient with me and Penelope."

"Yes, you are one lucky lady! I love the way he loves you," I tell her honestly. I wasn't a fan of Kyle's for a while. After he walked out on Max, she found out she was pregnant and didn't have the heart to tell him. He crushed her, and she was willing to raise the baby on her own. Thank God they both came to their senses. Kyle begged for her back, and they've been inseparable ever since.

I have to admit, watching the two of them together makes me yearn for the same thing. My only downfall is that I can't let my guard down. My fear stands in the way of my happiness."

"Oh! I forgot to tell you—guess who texted me last night?"

Max sits up in her chair. "Who?" she asks excitedly.

"Remember I told you about that guy Jax from last week at Starbucks?"

"Yeah!"

She is going to kill me if I leave her hanging any longer. "Well, we are meeting up for drinks tonight! He was one smokin' piece of ass. I just pray he's not a douche like that other jokester."

Max laughs. "Oh my God! For his sake, I hope not either! To be a fly on that wall! Whatcha wearing?"

I look down, waving my hand up and down my

body at my white blouse and black work pants. "This. I'm going there straight after I leave here," I explain. "This is *not* a date. This is a get-to-know-you, see-if-you-pass-inspection-for-a-first-date meeting," I say, watching Max's face contort, making me chuckle.

She stands up and heads toward the door. "Kins, you are too much! Call me if you need an out. I'm here for you!" she yells back.

I turn on Pandora and settle in for a long day of work.

I look up from the knock on my door. Great. It's Junior. I was finally digging myself out of my crappy morning mood, and here comes Mr. Debbie Downer. "What, Junior?" I snap.

He looks a little out of place and uncomfortable, bouncing from one foot to the other. This can't be good. "I just wanted to come apologize for this morning and see if you wanted to grab some lunch."

My mouth drops open slightly. There he goes again

—making me speechless! "Apology accepted, Junior. But there's no need for a pity lunch," I inform him, returning to my paperwork.

"Come on, Kinsey! I'm trying here. It's not a pity lunch. Honestly, everyone else is busy, so you are my last resort. Think of it as a pity lunch for me." Is he freaking serious?

I can tell he's making an attempt at a joke, but it's a poor one at my expense, not his. It might actually be some fun, though. It's time to get down to the nitty-gritty and find out who Mr. Junior really is!

"Geez, thanks," I reply, rolling my eyes. "Okay, but you're buying!"

He cracks a smile in relief. Hmm. He's kind of cute when he's vulnerable. I shut everything down, grab my jacket off the back of my chair, and lock my office behind me.

"So, where you taking me?" I ask.

I feel the eyes of our coworkers following us. Some seem surprised and others seem intrigued as to why we are walking out together. I laugh to myself, because I feel the same damn way. This guy rubs me in every possible wrong way. Sometimes it's electrifying, and sometimes it's just downright annoying as fuck.

"I figured we can go down to that little deli that Max and Elise are always talking about. I haven't been there yet. I am dying for a pastrami on rye. You ever been?" he asks.

I wave goodbye to Elise as we pass Kyle's office. She was moved up to his assistant a couple of months back, and her eyes practically bug out of her face. Aww, man! Here we go. I'm not ready for interrogation to come down on me later. I'm sure Max and Elise will be blowing my phone up in no time.

Junior unlocks his car from a distance. I roll my eyes. Of course he has a brand new Cadillac. I wouldn't expect anything less.

"Wait, did you just get this?" I direct his attention to his car.

He smiles proudly. "Yup, just a couple of days ago. It's the 2016 Cadillac ATS-V Coupe. I'm a sucker for a Cadi. You like it?" Huh, I gotta pay more attention to my surroundings.

Figures he would ask that. "Yeah, it's nice. Now maybe upgrade that pissy attitude, and you might score a chick," I tell him. Junior snorts.

We slide in and buckle up. I love the smell of leather in a new car. It's just does things to me.

"Does it ever occur to you that I don't want to just 'score' a chick? Maybe I'm looking for a bit more depth than the normal guy. Maybe I'm waiting around for the right woman to come along. Who the fuck wants to waste their time with the wrong one?"

Huh. Interesting. "So what you're saying is that you would rather jerk off than get some pussy?"

He looks disgusted. "One, that is correct. And two, clean that gutter mouth. Damn, woman! Were you raised in a barn or what?" he asks, laughing to himself. "No, I think you just like the reaction from it—am I right?"

I smirk without responding. He just chuckles.

We pull up to the café, and it's packed as usual.

He opens the front door for me. "Thanks. And to answer your question, I come here with the girls a lot.

Their BLTs are to die for."

We wait in line awkwardly. I can tell he doesn't do the whole lunch-date-with-single-girls-as-friends thing, so it's clear I'm going to have to control this conversation. We order our food and sit down at a small, quaint table in the corner.

"So tell me, sweet cheeks, do you even date?" I ask.

He looks away from me. "Not really. I haven't come into contact with anyone worth dating."

I try to gain his attention back. "But how are you supposed to get to know someone if you're not interacting with them? Sometimes things take time, and you need to plant the seed for it to grow," I inform him. Man, I'm feeling all philosophical and shit.

He shrugs his shoulders. "I think I'll just know."

The café worker comes over to drop the food off to our table. "Thank you," Junior says to her. She smiles back flirtatiously.

"So Kinsey, tell me why *you* haven't settled down yet."

I finish chewing this delicious bite and take a sip of my iced tea. "I guess I really haven't been looking. I'm actually having drinks with someone tonight after work. You know—getting to know someone before I decide if they're no good," I tell him, teasing.

He thinks about that for a moment. "So who's the guy?"

"His name is Jax. I met him at Starbucks last week. He was smooth in his approach, something I don't see a lot, so I'm going to see what he's all about," I answer.

"Where does he work?"

I take another sip of my tea. "I'm not too sure. He mentioned some law firm, but I can't remember the name. It was too early in the morning, and I hadn't had my coffee yet."

He nods, completely understanding that. Us people at Saunders Agency love our coffee.

"So, this is a date then," he says as more of a statement than a question.

I halt all eating and throw my pointer finger up. "Um, no. This is *not* a date. He hasn't earned a date yet. A date includes sexy dress attire, romance, and the possibility of a first kiss. This is simply to see if there's any sort of chemistry or if he falls in the friend zone or loser/creeper zone," I tell him proudly.

Sure, I've had my share of one-night stands. The guys were *always* smokin' hot, and I *always* knew there would never be a future. That's where the playing field becomes level for men and woman. If you go in knowing there's no possibility and you're okay with it, then it's just two consensual adults having a good time. There's nothing wrong with that.

Junior chuckles while finishing his sandwich. "Wow, you really have this thought out, don't you?"

"Damn straight! I'm not going to be one of those sappy, broken-hearted chicks who sobs while watching *The Notebook* and eating Ben and Jerry's. Nope. That is not me!" I tell him.

He studies me carefully. I'm not so sure I like this. "What happened to you? Who broke your heart?" he asks.

Shit! There is no way I'm opening up this can of worms with *him*. "Listen, sweet cheeks—you're getting too heavy on me. Let's save this conversation for never," I say, standing up to signal that it's time to go. "We need to get back."

As soon as I get back to my office, I am bombarded by Elise and Max. They make sure to close the door behind them so I am locked in and have no way out.

"*So*, how was your lunch?" Max questions with a huge shit-eating grin.

I roll my eyes. Yes, I do this a lot, but it's either roll my eyes or stomp my feet like a two-year-old. "Don't get any ideas, you two! We just had a meal together. We freaking live together already. What's the big deal?"

Elise giggles, having fun watching it go down between us. I direct my attention at her. "And you—you just *had* to go and open your mouth!"

She holds up her hands in defense. "If I hadn't told Max, someone else in the office would have. Believe me; I heard the whispers."

I lean back into my chair. Great. That's all I need;

my coworkers gossiping about me.

"So, how was it?" Max asks again impatiently.

"It actually wasn't that bad. When he removes the stick from his ass, he's not terrible to be around," I tell them.

"See, I told you! There's a side to him that he rarely shows. I tell him all the time he needs to loosen up. He's really kind-hearted and very gentle. You should see the way he interacts with Penelope. I just wish Kyle and him could resolve their issues. I've tried so hard to get them to talk, but they're both so stubborn," Max explains.

"So, Kyle's never even told you what their deal is?" I ask.

Max exhales loudly. "Honestly, I don't even think Kyle really knows."

"Yeah, I've asked Jeff, and he has no idea either. He thinks it has to do with the girl, Mary, that Junior was close with until Kyle screwed her brains out and made her all psycho," Elise says.

Huh. I bet I can get the reason out of him. It might take a couple glasses of red wine, but I'm pretty good at coercing the truth out of people. "But they were so young when that happened."

"I know, tell me about it!" Max says. She gets out of the chair and walks toward the door. "We have a meeting at two. Make sure you bring all your notes on the Jefferson proposal. Mr. Saunders is going to want to go over everything in full detail. Be prepared. It's going to be a long meeting," she informs before walking out.

Elise follows suit, but before she heads back, she turns to me. "You know I love you, right?"

My hearts melts a bit. "And I love you too, Elise! Even though you blew my spot up!" I tease.

We both laugh. I wouldn't trade my girls for anything in the world. They keep me sane, which is a really hard thing to do, because I am bat-shit crazy. I admit it!

CHAPTER THREE

Junior

Lunch with Kinsey was interesting to say the least. I actually enjoyed her company. I seem to be saying that a lot now. I don't know why I haven't tried to get to know her before. I guess that's a fault of mine: shutting people out before I even give them a chance. Who the hell wants to go through life vulnerable and scared of being hurt? Not me, that's for sure.

I saw the same thing with Kinsey. It's like she puts on this front to deflect people from her vulnerable side just like I do. I never really took the time to notice this before, but now she kind of makes a little more sense. I always thought she was just rude and crazy with no filter, and even though she refused to discuss her past with me, I now know there is a reason behind her madness.

I look up to see Jeff plopping himself down in the chair in front of me. "What's up, bro?" he says with a huge smirk on his face. Aww great. Here we go; this can't be good.

"What's up, man?"

"So, you and Kins, huh?" he questions, digging.

I throw my hands up in the air. "Dude, really? We just went out for lunch!"

He chuckles. "Okay, okay! No need to get all defensive. Since when do you guys go out for lunch, though?"

He is unbelievable. "Since I was a total douche to her this morning. I felt bad. So I took her to lunch. That's it. Nothing more, nothing less. How's that for an answer?"

I really want to smack the grin off of his face right about now. "That's a good answer, man. All I'm gonna say is that it's about damn time! Even though she's irritating as shit, she's still hot. Why not give it a go?" he suggests.

Now he's pushing it. "Didn't we already have this discussion? I'm not fucking the girl! She may be hot, but she's not my type. Anyways, she's going out on some date or whatever tonight," I add, no idea why that even came out of my mouth.

"Oh yeah? Where to?"

I think back for a moment. "I don't think she said."

"Well hey, Elise and I are stopping by your brother's after work to see Penelope. You wanna come?" he asks.

"I would love to, but I gotta stay late tonight and catch up on some work."

Jeff stands up to head out. "Alright, man. Don't go giving yourself an ulcer from working too hard."

By the time I look down at my watch, it's quarter to seven. I shut my door earlier and haven't opened it up since. I had two conference calls with clients and only one bathroom break. I'm doing my damnedest to keep my mind off of Kinsey. I don't know what the hell my problem is, but ever since last night, she's been popping up in my thoughts. It's actually driving me insane.

She's out with that guy Jax right now. I wish I would have asked her where she was meeting him. What if he turns out to be a creep? Maybe I should call her or text her to make sure she is doing okay. I pick up my phone, then immediately throw it back down as if it's on fire. I shake my head. What the fuck am I doing? She goes on dates all the time, so why am I so concerned now?

No, no, no. I whisper to myself. I'm going to just go home and hit the sack. I am exhausted, and I'm just not thinking straight. I close everything up for the night and head out. I walk out into the chilly night's air and zip my jacket up to my neck as I watch my breath in front of me. I'm not ready for winter quite yet. That means more nights at home with no one to share them with. Shit can get lonely.

I pull into the garage and take the elevator up to my floor. I wonder if Kinsey is home yet. I open the door, but before I step in, I check for heels. I'll be damned if I trip over her pumps again. No heels. Which means no Kinsey.

I set my briefcase on the kitchen counter and grab a glass of water before heading to my room. I immediately strip all my clothes off and jump into a nice, hot shower. I throw my sweats on, and I lay in bed. After watching two episodes of *Law and Order,* it's now ten o'clock, and no Kinsey. Now I'm starting to get worried. I should have called her earlier. What if something really happened to her? I throw my covers off of me, grab my phone, and head out to the kitchen.

I pour myself a shot of Patrón in hopes of shutting my brain off—or maybe to help cloud my judgement even more, because I have no idea what I'm doing. Since when do I give a flying fuck about what Kinsey does? She's always been like the annoying sister I never wanted, so what's changed?

I hear the keys rustle at the door. I feel relieved that she's home. She walks through the door, kicks off her heels —leaving them in the middle of the walkway—and then jumps when she looks up.

"What the fuck are you doing? You scared the shit out of me!" she hollers.

I take another sip of my wine. "I was worried about you. Where the hell have you been? It's almost eleven o'clock," I growl, sounding like a nagging boyfriend.

She looks at me as though I have two heads. "Um,

since when have I ever had to answer to *you*? You sound crazy right now. Go to bed, Junior," she instructs as she walks behind me to grab a glass of water.

Man, maybe she is right. I do sound crazy right now. I *feel* crazy right now. "You're right. I just wanted to make sure you got home safe. That guy could have been a creeper or even worse—a rapist or something."

"Well, he wasn't. We have a date this Saturday. He made the cut," she informs as she leaves the kitchen and walks to her room.

A sharp twinge jabs me from deep within. I don't know why I feel affected by her comment, but it irks me for some reason—just as bad as those shoes left in the middle of the walkway do. I just need some sleep. It's clear I'm reacting like a lunatic due to sleep deprivation.

My alarm goes off; shrieking in my ear. I slam my hand over it to shut it up. My eyes feel dry and sore. I swear I barely slept. I tossed and turned all night long. My brain wouldn't shut down!

I wipe the crusties from my eyes and drag myself out of bed. This is all Kinsey's fault. I don't know what she did to me, but I can't get her out of my goddamn mind. It's making me sick. I need to go back to my rude, assholish self. I was way better off; at least I could sleep.

I get dressed and creep out of my room. I don't want any run-ins this morning. I would actually like to avoid her at all costs. I skip the coffee, grab my briefcase, and head out the door. I feel relief wash over me as I head to my car. No smart mouth, and no embarrassment to fend off.

I get to the office, and it's pretty low key; the employees aren't expected in for another forty-five minutes. I go to the breakroom to grab some coffee. I should have stopped at Starbucks, but I wouldn't want to run into Kinsey and her new man, so I drove past it.

Bridgette, one of my editors, walks in. "Hey, Junior. Wow, you look like you didn't get a wink of sleep!" she comments. Awesome. Is it that freaking noticeable?

"I didn't," I reply. "But thanks for noticing," I tell her before walking out of the kitchen.

Bridgette can be very blunt sometimes. That's what I've always liked about her, but it sucks when it's at my expense. I've thought about asking her out for dinner before. She's cute. Not really my complete type, but she's smart and really knows her shit. I just couldn't look past the fact that she works with me and my dick doesn't stir when being in her presence.

I may sound like a douche, but like I told Kinsey yesterday, I'm not going to waste my time unless I'm one hundred percent into it. I walk past Max's office. Kinsey and her seem to be in deep conversation. Max waves to me, and Kinsey looks back toward me with humor in her eyes.

I make it safely to my office, but as soon as I log into my computer, I hear a knock at my door. I look up and Kinsey is leaning against the doorway. "So, where were you this morning?" she questions.

"I had to come in early. Why, what's up?" I wonder.

She squints her eyes. "I made coffee for you, but when I got up, you were gone. What was up with last night?"

I was hoping she wouldn't go there. "You told me

you were meeting up with this dude for the first time, and it was late. I just wanted to make sure you got home OK. Is that such a crime?"

"Coming from you? Yes," she giggles. "You looked like you were about to go ham on me! But thanks for watching out for me," she finishes with a wink.

This damn girl. "Yeah, it won't happen again," I tell her.

"Okay, whatever you say, sweet cheeks," she taunts before walking away.

I don't know what it is with her, but she constantly gets under my skin.

The rest of the week passes by quickly, and it's finally Friday. Nothing unusual or exciting happened. I did my best to avoid Kinsey at all costs. She came into my office the other day to see if I wanted to go out for lunch, but I passed. I made up a quick excuse to get her out of my office.

The way I went off on her earlier this week messed

my whole head up. I needed some space. I felt suffocated with thoughts of her, and I needed to create some distance —get back to my old self that thought the sight of her was just annoying as fuck.

Tonight's not going to help any, because we'll all be at Jeff and Elise's house, hanging out and drinking together. That means hours of being in the same room with this girl. I'm just going to do my best to keep my distance.

I decide to leave work early today so I can take a nap. The hours I have been putting in this week have completely drained me of energy. I think it takes more energy to avoid Kinsey than it takes to cross paths with her. I need to rest before I go into the gauntlet tonight.

It's quiet and peaceful in the apartment. I dose off quickly, but when I am awoken, it's by Kinsey standing over me, shaking me. I look around, confused. Am I dreaming? I look up at her to ask her why she's in my room, but instead of allowing the words to flow out of my mouth, I feel my hard dick under my sweats.

Yup. Just the sight of her makes my dick hard. Shit. I look at her through my groggy eyes. She's absolutely beautiful, and without another thought, I grab her hand and pull her down to me. She struggles for a moment, asking me what the fuck I'm doing, but all thoughts and questions fly out the door when our lips touch.

She melds perfectly into me. Her plush lips feel amazingly soft against mine. She opens for me willingly as I glide my tongue into her mouth. A small moan escapes her, going straight to my cock. I run my fingers through the back of her hair and tug gently as our tongues dance together.

Everything about her is so tantalizing: her smell, her skin, her sweet moans. I can't seem to get enough. The energy surrounding us is on fire. She's engulfing me with her electrifying aura, and I can't seem to get enough. I'm tangled in her web, but I have no urge to break free.

Her palms lie on my bare chest; her fingernails digging into me. Just as I'm about to shift her body over mine, she disconnects from me and pushes away. I want to beg for her to come back.

"Junior, what the *fuck* are we doing?" she questions, running her hands through her hair.

I now feel nothing but cold air hitting my stifling hot body. Shit! What did I just do? Kinsey stands up, pacing in front of my bed. I sit up, trying to make sense of all this. Did this really just happen? "Why are you in my room?" I question.

"Because I was calling for you and you wouldn't wake up!" she explains. Okay, time to play it cool. I've never been in this position before.

I get out of my bed and head toward my bathroom. "You woke me out of a good dream. Don't take the kiss too personal. I was out of it. I wasn't thinking clearly," I lie. I don't bother to turn toward her as I'm speaking, but when I turn on the bathroom light, I swear I see Kyle's reflection in the mirror, not mine. Damn, what was I thinking? I catch her reflection, and she looks hurt and then completely enraged.

"You're a fucking asshole, you know that?" she screeches. "I swear, if you come near me again, I'll rip your balls off and feed them to you, fuckface!"

I watch her storm out of the room and slam my door. I jump at the loud backlash it causes. I really pissed her off. This is not good. A pissed-off Kinsey is like a hungry tiger; she wants to rip my head off. I'm at a loss for words. Most of the time I can't even stand to be near her, but then I go and kiss her? What the hell is *wrong* with me?

I get into a cool shower before taking off to Jeff's. With my luck, Kinsey will already be gone. I'm going to need some backup. I just don't trust her. I shake my head as I throw my T-shirt on. Man, what a mess. If I was in my right state of mind, that would have never happened. I had just woken up, and I allowed the feeling in my cock to take the lead. Never a smart idea. Never.

I pull up to Jeff and Elise's, and the first car I see is Kinsey's. I can only imagine what she has told the girls. I'm probably going to be bombarded with nasty looks and shit talking. I take a deep breath and head in.

Max is the first one to greet me. "Junior!" she yells, rushing at me with a big hug. "I'm so glad you're here!"

"Hey, careful now. You're gonna break me," I joke.

"Penelope has been waiting to see you."

I look ahead. "Is that right?" I see Penelope sitting in her high chair with Cheerios all over the place. I run over to her and kiss her chunky little cheeks. She laughs and it fills the room.

Elise greets me with a kiss on the cheek, and I say what's up to the guys. Kinsey is sitting at the kitchen table, refusing to even acknowledge my existence. I can see the steam rising off of her body in angry waves. It doesn't seem like the girls know a thing. At least I know she has kept our kiss to herself. I can relax just a bit. We never really spoke much before, so this shouldn't be any different.

The only problem is it *is* different. Every time my eyes drift over to her, all I can picture is that kiss. I keep having to shake myself from the memory so my dick doesn't go hard in front of everyone. That would be the conversation of the night.

"Beer, bro?" Jeff asks, holding out a Heineken to me.

I grab the bottle from him and take a huge swig. Boy, I needed this. Max walks over and plops Penelope in my arms. I quickly put the beer down and start tickling her. I love hearing this laugh. It can make any bad day good. I look up and catch Kinsey watching. She quickly turns away.

"What's up with Kins? Why does she look all uptight and shit?" Jeff asks.

I shrug my shoulders. "I don't know. She's always high strung."

Jeff chuckles. "True that! But this seems a little different." I pretend to ignore his last statement.

I bring Penelope to the living room and set her down next to her box of toys. It's time for Uncle Junior to get his playtime in. Max comes over and sits down on the couch, facing us with her glass of wine.

"She's getting so big, isn't she?"

Penelope hums while biting on her plastic blue ring. "Yes. Before you know it, she's going to be walking. I need to stop by more often. So when's the next Saunders baby?" I ask Max.

She blows out a deep breath. "Um, yeah, I think we're gonna hold off for a while. I feel like I was pregnant forever! I'm enjoying having my body back!" Max jokes. Her voice suddenly turns to a whisper as she adds, "Hey, what's up with Kinsey? Did you guys get into an argument or something?" The rest of the bunch are in the kitchen chowing down on some snacks.

"No, why do you ask?"

"She just seems a little off. She told me she was going to wake you up from your nap to see if you wanted to drive here together, but then you guys drove separate. So I thought maybe something happened," Max finishes.

Shit. I really hate lying. "She woke me up, but I told her to go ahead. I had to jump in the shower."

She thinks about my answer for a minute, then laughs at Penelope as the baby shrieks to get my attention. Yup, she's learning early how to demand a guy's attention. Of course I can't help but give it to her.

"Max, tell me something—what's Kinsey's story?" I question. Kinsey was so quick to shut me out; I know there's a reason behind it.

"Her story is hers to tell. Why don't you ask her?"

I figured she would say that. "I tried, and she shut

me down."

Max giggles. "Of course she did. Keep trying. Don't give up," she tells me.

I glance up toward the others, laughing like hyenas, and my eyes draw to Kinsey like a magnet. I guess I really never took the time to notice, but she is absolutely gorgeous.

I snap out of it and try to shake my thoughts, but Max catches me staring at Kinsey. I quickly look away, pretending to look at something else, but I can't fool her. Max looks back at me with an all-knowing smirk. Damn. She caught me.

"Any dates lately?" she asks.

Elise joins us. "What did I miss?"

"I just asked Junior here if he has had any dates lately," Max explains.

They both wait patiently for my answer. "No, no dates. I was thinking about asking Bridgette out, though."

They both look at each other, then back to me. "Bridgette is nice. I like her," Elise comments.

Max has a-whole-nother opinion. "She's not for

you, Junior. Besides, you two work together; what happens if things go south?"

The pot calling the kettle black. "I'd like to remind you that you also worked with my brother, and look at the two of you now."

She softens a bit. "Yes, I am very aware of that, but things did go south for a while. We almost didn't make it. The thought of seeing him at work after all that crap was completely debilitating. I don't want you to have to go through that. Besides I think there's someone out there that's perfect for you; you just haven't realized it yet," she clarifies.

The wheels are turning in her head, and I'm afraid to know what she actually is trying to say. There's a hidden agenda in those words. I can see it in her mischievous eyes, but I choose to ignore it.

The whole rest of the night was interesting. Penelope and I played so hard that she knocked out quickly. Kyle and I kept our distance, and Kinsey wouldn't look at me most of the night, but when she did, it was the death stare. After this long week, my bed is now calling my name.

It's late morning, and I finally drag my butt out of bed. I'm in need of some major coffee, but I'm a little hesitant about walking outside of my room. I listen at the door to see if I hear any movement. It sounds quiet, so maybe the coast is clear. I open the door quietly and head out to the kitchen. There's no Kinsey in sight. *Phew!*

Usually on Saturday mornings I have coffee waiting for me, and I hear music blasting from her room, but not today. It's dead silent with no life. I guess I never realized how much spunk she brings into a room. She fills it with life and chaos. I've always been annoyed by this, but this morning I'm sort of missing it.

I just need to shake that kiss and get my mind on something else, like work. I'm going into the office. I'll grab some coffee on the way. Being there always passes the time. This is how I learned the business so fast at a young age; I put women on the backburner and concentrated on becoming successful. Now I'm wondering if that might have been a mistake.

I look down at my watch, and it's now quarter to four. I've been in the office for about five hours, but all I can seem to think about is Kinsey's date tonight. Is she meeting him there, or is he picking her up from our apartment? I can't remember if she mentioned a time, but if I leave now, I can make sure I'm around to meet this guy, see what he's all about.

CHAPTER FOUR

Kinsey

I'm looking forward to tonight's date with Jax. We really hit it off when we had drinks last Tuesday night. He actually enjoyed my sarcastic sense of humor—unlike some people I know. I'm doing the whole first-date-shebang! I have my favorite sexy black dress, my hot pink pumps, and my matching bold lipgloss on. This girl is gonna turn heads tonight! I have to keep the men on their toes.

I look at my phone; it's nearly six. He should be here at any moment. At first, I was a little hesitant about having him pick me up at the apartment, but after that fucked-up kiss with Junior last night, I decided screw it. He needs to know it didn't affect me. Although, I just wish I could believe those words myself.

The truth is, I can't stop thinking about it. Junior was the last person in the world I wanted to kiss, but when it happened, it was breathtaking. Everything about the kiss was hot as hell, but what scared me the most is that I wanted more. I wanted him to touch every part of me; to feel him inside of me. That's why I pushed him away. I freaked. I allowed myself to let go just for a split moment, and this is what I get in return—thoughts of him all day long.

I think that's why I'm looking forward to this date so much. I need a distraction. I'm hoping that being with Jax again will completely wipe Junior out of my thoughts. Then we can go back to being strangers in the same apartment.

I hear the door buzzer go off. Jax must be here. I check myself one last time before heading out. I leave my room to let him in, but Junior has already beat me to the punch. My stomach tightens just a bit as our eyes lock. I quickly disconnect and walk by him to greet Jax at the door.

I can feel Junior's eyes boring into my back. A sudden heat creeps over my skin. I have less than ten seconds to get myself together. I am relieved once Jax is in my presence. I give him an intimate hug, just holding on long enough for Junior to get uncomfortable. He clearly has no qualms about watching.

Jax clears his throat, then walks to Junior to introduce himself. "Hey, man. I'm Jax," he says, holding out his hand.

Junior reciprocates. "I'm Junior, Kinsey's roommate," he says stiffly.

Jax looks back to me. "Well, nice to meet you. Kinsey never mentioned a roommate."

I shrug my shoulders. Yeah, I guess I did forget. "You ready?" I ask.

He smiles and nods his head. "Later, man," Jax says to Junior. Junior just nods, looking displeased. Good. That's what his ass gets!

We head down to Jax's car, and he opens the door for me. I haven't had this happen in a while. I guess chivalry isn't completely dead. His car's nice, or maybe I should say SUV. Though, for a lawyer I would have expected a Mercedes or Jaguar, something sporty and cocky. I guess this suits him.

"So, where are you taking me?" I ask.

We pull out of the parking garage. "Do you like hibachi?" he questions.

"I do!"

"Good, because that's where we're going. I know the owner pretty well, so he's setting us up a nice, private table," Jax informs me.

Okay! I can definitely do the VIP treatment. So far, so good.

"How was your week? I would have texted more, but I'm knee-deep in court cases. So I apologize," he says.

"No worries. I completely understand the crazy job thing. Have you always wanted to be a lawyer?"

He keeps his eyes on the road. "Actually, yes. My father is a lawyer, and my grandfather was a lawyer. So it kind of runs in the family."

"What did your mom do?"

"She actually stayed home and raised my sisters and I," he replies.

Oh no! Sisters? Ugh. I hate sisters. "How many sisters do you have?"

Please only say one. Please only say one. "I have

three," he answers. Shit! "I'm the baby of the family. Two are married, and the other one has a partner."

"Partner as in a woman?"

"Yup. That would be right."

Pretty cool. "How are your parents with the whole thing?"

He looks over at me and smiles. "My parents love Jan. My sister, Kayla, was always a tomboy. Just never fit in with the girls. We were pretty tight growing up. I guess she was more like an older brother to me," he says, chuckling. "But my parents always knew. I guess we got lucky with the unconditional love thing. Not everyone gets that."

"No, you're very right about that. My best friend, Maxine, had some pretty shitty parents growing up."

Max's mother was never around, and her father was an abusive drunk.

We turn into the restaurant parking lot. "I'm sorry to hear that. That sounds horrible. So, what about your parents; what were they like?" he asks.

I can't help but smile brightly. "I got lucky. My

parents are incredible. My mother owns a clothing store back in South Carolina, and my father works with Max's brother, Luke, at the marina."

"Any brothers or sisters?"

"Nope. I am a spoiled only child," I say with a giggle.

He smirks. "Oh boy! I think that means I'm in trouble, huh?"

I zip my mouth and throw away the pretend key. Jax laughs. I'm actually really enjoying him so far, and we haven't even gotten to the actual date. He is a major hottie! Normally I would be begging to get groped like a horny teenager by now, but my mind keeps drifting to Junior. It's kind of a major cock block. Maybe if I get some drinks in me, this will change.

"Ready?" he asks.

I nod. We get out of the SUV and head to the door. The restaurant is extremely busy. Families and kids are packed in the waiting area like sardines. Jax walks right up to the hostess and announces our arrival. I see the blush creep into her cheeks as he smiles that dashing smile at her.

Poor girl. She was a goner at hello.

She immediately walks us back to our table. It's most definitely private. We have our own hibachi grill and chef just for us in the back. I like this. I could get used to this kind of treatment.

"So tell me, how do you know the owner?"

The waiter comes immediately to get our drink order and then leaves us.

"I helped him out in a matter a while back. Him and his wife are great people, and the food is amazing," he explains.

"I am freaking starving!"

He grins as we sit here in silence for a moment, just looking at each other. I really want to stick my tongue out at him, but I think that might ruin the moment. "How is a woman as beautiful as you still single?" he asks.

Shit! I hate this question with a passion. "Would you run if I told you I turn into a crazy stage-five clinger?"

He laughs. "Oh yeah? Check please—" he says jokingly. "No, really though. What's your deal?"

Man, I seem to get this damn question a lot. "To be

honest, I don't settle. I won't settle. I like to have fun and enjoy time with someone. Once you go around putting a title on things, it ruins it. I would rather keep things light, and I guess it's been an issue for some," I finish, hoping he's not going to run the other way.

He contemplates my answer for a moment. "I admire that. I believe in friendship first, but maybe mixed with a little romance to keep you on your toes."

I can breathe a little easier now. "I think I can handle that," I tell him with a smirk.

The waiter comes over with our drinks. We order while the grill heats up.

The rest of the dinner goes by great. We chatted some more and laughed a lot. I can't remember the last time I laughed this much; my stomach literally hurts.

I look at my phone. It's already ten, and I have three missed calls from Max and one text from Elise. I don't know if they're worried or just want the scoop—probably a little bit of both.

"You good?" Jax asks, eyeing my phone as we pull into my parking garage.

I giggle. "It's just my girlfriends blowing up my phone. You know, the norm," I shrug.

He nods, completely understanding. "Can I walk you to your door? I want to make sure you get in OK. Don't want anyone to steal you," he jokes with a wink.

Good move, Jax. Good move. "Sure, but just to let you know—if I get stolen, I think they'll throw me right back. My mouth can be very dangerous sometimes," I tell him, giving him my sexiest come-hither smile. Maybe one kiss won't hurt. I gotta test drive the car before I buy it, right?

We ride up the elevator in silence—an energy-filled intense silence. The thought of me being with Jax on one side of the door and having Junior on the other side is throwing me off a bit.

Jax grabs my hand before we exit. When we get to my door, he smoothly goes in for a kiss before I have time to overthink it. Man, he's good! His lips are velvety soft, and his tongue tastes of mint—though I don't recall him chewing any gum or mints. Damn, Kins, get it together! Your tongue is down this guy's throat, and this is all you can think of? Ugh.

I feel his hand on my waist as he brings me closer to him. His other hand glides through my hair. Okay, this is nice, but it's getting a little too intense. I put my hands against his chest with just a little pressure applied. He slowly rescinds.

"I'm sorry, I got a little carried away," Jaxs admits shyly. Shyness looks cute on him.

I remove my hands from his chest, giving us space. "Thank you for the date. I had a great time."

"Can I see you again?" he asks.

I tuck my hair behind my ear. "Yes, I would love that."

He leans down to kiss my cheek. "Good. I'll text you this week."

I open the door quietly so I don't wake Junior. I make sure to line my shoes up nicely next to the door so I don't get his wrath brought down on me tomorrow. I've had a little too much to drink, so Advil and water is a must. I turn off the main kitchen light after chugging down the pills. I suddenly jump back because Junior is standing in front of me like a creepo.

"What the fuck, Junior?" I yell, my heart beating like crazy. He walks around me and grabs a glass from the cupboard.

"I couldn't sleep," he tells me. Yeah, okay.

"Did you hear me come in?" I ask.

He pours some water and downs it. "No, why?" he looks at me with dead, cold eyes. Ouch. I shiver and cross my arms over my chest.

"Okay, I'm going to bed," I announce.

I turn to walk away. "How was the date?" he asks. Bingo. I knew it. He couldn't sleep, because his ass was waiting up for me just like the last time. But why? Why does he care?

"So, this is it? We're all of a sudden talking now? Talking like that kiss never happened?" I question, putting my hands on my hips. He was a total dick last night, and now he thinks he has a right to know how my damn date was? Oh hell no!

I walk up to him with my pointer finger out. "And what the hell was that all about earlier? Since when do you sit around, waiting to meet my dates?" I screech.

"Since you bring your dates to the apartment. I wanted him to know that you are not a single woman living alone. You barely know the guy, Kinsey. He could turn out to be some killing-psycho-rapist! So you can thank me now for saving your ass!" he growls. What the—?

I shake my head. I don't know whether to argue or laugh. He sounds absolutely ridiculous. "Well, thank you, but he is amazing. So I don't think I'll be needing you," I purposely tell him before walking away and leaving him hanging. I think I may have heard his jaw drop.

I'm woken up at the crack-ass of dawn by Max calling my phone multiple times. I want to throw it against my wall. I look at my clock and the freaking thing says nine-thirty in the morning. It's Sunday, for God's sake! Is she out of her mind?

I hit answer. "I'm going to kill you!" I bark.

She giggles. "Well if you would have called me last night, I wouldn't be calling you now."

I slam my arm over my eyes. "Okay, okay. I'm sorry. I should have called. I got home late, and I was tired. Then Junior got out of bed to grill me on how my date went!" I tell her, forgetting I haven't told her about the weird kiss.

"Wait, what? Why would he do that? Oh ... wait ... that's what that look was all about! Kins, I hate to tell ya, but I think Junior's got it bad for you," she informs me.

I take my hand off my eyes and sit up. "Why do you think that?"

"I caught him staring at you last night. The look in his eyes said it all. He caught me catching him!" she laughs. "No, but seriously, he asked about you too. He wanted to know what your deal was," she finishes.

Now I'm freaked out. "And did you tell him?" I worry.

"Of course not!" she says, sounding insulted. I should have known she wouldn't rat me out. "I told him you had a story, but it's yours to tell."

I release the breath I was holding. "Okay, so—don't be mad. But we sort of kissed the other night before we came to the house," I admit, cringing, waiting for her to spaz out on me.

"Kins! Are you fucking serious? Spill it now!" she demands.

I slam my body back down on my bed. I'm gonna have to lie down for this one. "I went to wake him up, to see if he wanted to ride with me, and he just pulled me down for a kiss."

I hear her squealing. "*And?*"

"Max, I'm not going to lie—he is a fucking good-ass kisser! I almost couldn't contain myself. I wanted to jump on him like a bitch in heat, but I stopped myself. I had to. Then he went back to his asshole self. He told me he was out of it and that's why he kissed me. I swear, I wanted to rip his fucking head off after that! And yesterday he waited at the kitchen counter so he could meet Jax. He's just so damn aggravating!" I finally finish.

"Oh my God, Kins. I want to smack him for being an ass, but not for nothing, he was probably caught off guard, just as you were. I knew something was going on! The energy was just so off. So, now what?" she asks.

Man, I wish I knew. "No freaking idea! I'm going to go make myself some coffee before he gets back from the gym, and hide out in my room for the rest of the day." Maybe this is a bit childish, but I could give two shits.

Max laughs. "Okay, well if you need to get away, you are always welcome here."

"Thanks, but I'm about to bury myself under the covers for the rest of the day. And thanks for waking me up, ass!" I tell her.

We hang up, and I rush to the kitchen. I think I may have less than an hour before he comes through the door. Normally, I'm all about torturing him; it's fun as hell. But I'm not about to get myself stuck in that situation again. No way. I'd rather eat glass.

I drift in and out of sleep all day while watching Lifetime movies. I can't remember the last time I had a day like this. I *so* needed this! It's now eight o'clock, and I need to get into the shower. I stink. Unfortunately, I don't have a bathroom connected to my room. I should have switched rooms when Max left, while I had the chance.

I open my door and creep out. Geez, this just feels

so wrong. Since when do I hide from a guy? I should be standing up straight and marching right out of my fucking door, not acting like a weak child. But then I remember the kiss—how I felt so vulnerable and open. I don't want to feel that again.

This hot shower does wonders for my body, especially after lying in bed all day. I soak it all up until the water turns cold, and then I drag my butt out. I wrap the towel around me tightly, then wipe the steam off the mirror with the edge of my hand. My face is flush with pink and hair dripping wet. I grab a second towel to wrap around my hair and open the door to head to my room, but when I step out, I ram right into Junior—*again*.

"Damn, Junior!" I screech this time, completely caught off guard. I hold onto my towel just a bit tighter. There's no way this sucker is coming loose.

He puts his hands up. "What the hell did *I* do? You ran into *me*."

"You sure about that?" I question. "If I didn't know any better, I would think you were standing here, waiting for me to come out," I suggest, totally baiting him.

He laughs. "Oh, now I'm a stalker in my own apartment? I didn't know there were rules on what time I'm allowed to come out of my bedroom," he finishes, walking around me toward the kitchen.

Ugh! He's so freaking aggravating! I stomp into my room and slam the door. I know, a little dramatic, but I had to take this frustration out on something! The worst part is seeing him in those sweatpants that sit just below his hips with his dark happy trail directing the way. So fucking sexy, and I hate it! I smack myself in the forehead.

Damn! There I go. What the fuck is *wrong* with me? This is Junior: stiff-as-fuck, irritating, mundane Junior! That's the only way I can explain him. But then he just had to throw in this wrench with that jaw-dropping kiss, *and* I just had to go like it.

My phone dings. I look at the text, and it's from Max.

"How's it going over there? Do I need to call the fire department yet?" she jokes. I roll my eyes.

"Not funny WHATSOEVER!" I type back.

"Lol! K, just checking up to make sure you two haven't killed each other or worse ... ended up in each other's bed!"

Oh, I am *so* gonna get her for this! "Stop worrying about me, and go bang your hubby!" I text back with fury.

She sends me a smiley face with a tongue sticking out.

I dry my body off and put on my night clothes. I sit down at my makeup station and begin to dry my damp hair. My mind wanders off to last night with Jax. I really couldn't have asked for a better first date. Our kiss would have actually been pretty perfect if my mind allowed my body to feel it. Second dates rarely happen for me; I always seem to find something wrong beforehand. Now I'm wondering if Jax is too good to be true; what the hell did I miss?

I have to admit—those hazel eyes are panty-dropper status; I just wish they were my panties that wanted to drop. Maybe I'm just getting more mature. Maybe my body is just telling me I need to slow down. Pfff! Who the hell am I trying to fool? Clearly myself, because my body is telling me to walk right into Junior's room, get on top of him, and ride him like a pony!

I slam my head down on the glass. I am one hot mess. Just stick a fork in me; I am done! I finish drying my hair and climb into bed. The back of my lids are the only thing I want to see.

CHAPTER FIVE

Junior

My pen smacks down on my desk over and over while my mind drifts off to thoughts of Kinsey. I feel clouded and sucked into a whirlwind full of her. How did this happen? When did I allow her to take over?

I hear a knock in the far distance. I finally get out of my mucky haze.

"Dude! Bro!" Jeff says, bringing me out of my stupor. I look up at him. "Wow, man. Where were you just now?" he asks, sitting down in the chair in front of me.

"Sorry, man. Just working," I lie. "What's up?"

Jeff looks fidgety and a little flush. "Are you sick?" I question.

He wipes the sheen of sweat off of his forehead with the back of his hand. "No. I need to talk to you about something," he explains. I wait for him to come out with it. "I've been thinking a lot, and I've realized that there's no way I could ever live without Elise in my life," he admits.

Oh no! I think I know where this is headed. "I'm ready to ask her to marry me."

I rub my hand over my face, trying to hold my feelings in. I'm proud of Jeff for making this decision. Elise is a great woman, and they are perfect for each other, but it doesn't stop me from feeling a little envious. I want this. I'm ready for a wife and kids. I just don't know how to open up to someone else. Mary was the last girl I allowed myself to feel anything for, but she chose Kyle over me. I was just a stepping stone for her. She didn't care about me or our friendship; she just used me. After feeling so small and unwanted, I never wanted to feel those feelings again, so I've shut myself off.

I've dated here and there. Nothing too crazy, but I think after hearing this, it's time I try to allow myself to feel again, to live. At this point, I'd rather hurt than feel nothing at all. Look where that's gotten me—nowhere.

I stand up and walk around my desk to give him a man-hug. "That's awesome, man! Really, I never thought this day would come. Did you pick out a ring yet?"

Jeff exhales. "Na, man. That's where you come in. I

was hoping you would come with me after work. I told Elise I was going out for a drink."

Wow. This is pretty cool. I wonder if he spoke to my brother about this yet. "Does Kyle know?" I ask.

He chuckles. "No, not yet. You would think I would have gone to him first since he's already been through this, but you're more practical. I thought if maybe I was making the wrong decision, you wouldn't be afraid to say so. Also, Kyle can't keep a secret from Max. It would kill him, and she would know something was up. I don't want to put him in that situation," he clarifies.

I laugh. Boy, is he right on that one. "I got you, man. Whatever you need, I'm here."

Jeff smiles excitedly. "Cool. Just meet me a Jared's at five thirty. I have to make sure Elise is gone before we leave," he tells me. Before he leaves my office, he turns to me. "Dude, you're next on the list! We gotta find you a woman!"

I wave him off. He's crazy if he thinks I'm going to allow him to find me someone. But it does dawn on me that I am "next on the list," so maybe Bridgette would be the safest route to go, for now. I shut the door to my office and walk over to hers. She's on the phone but waves me in.

I lean against the doorjamb just in case she says no and I need to make a quick getaway.

"Hey, Junior, what's up?" she asks.

Here it goes—it's time to man up. "Just was curious if maybe you wanted to get something to eat with me later this week?" Shit, shit, shit! She's totally going to say no.

Her eyes twinkle when she smiles. "Sure, I would love that! When would you like to go?"

"How about tomorrow after work? There's a new bar that opened up; it's a really chill place. I heard the food is great too," I tell her. My heart is pumping furiously.

"Okay, sounds good!"

This is my cue to leave. I wave goodbye; what an ass move. I'm totally going to see her again today. What am I going to do—wave? I'm totally rusty with this sort of shit. Maybe I should have asked her to meet me at the apartment so I could see the look on Kinsey's face.

Just slap me now. Did I really just think that? Why

the hell do I care about getting Kinsey jealous? I feel like this chick is going to drive me to therapy, and we only kissed once for Christ's sake! What the hell would have happened if had sex, like I wanted to in that moment? I think I would have been a goner. I'm staying clear of her, and that's my word! She's dangerous in every sort of way possible.

I pass Kyle's office. He looks swamped, but he calls me over when he catches a glimpse of me. What the hell does he want? I refuse to let him ruin my mood.

"Hey," I greet him.

He finishes his text quickly. "Hey, is something going on with Jeff? He looks a little out of it," Kyle pries. Nice try, little bro.

"I don't think so. He's probably just hungover, or maybe too much sex last night," I joke. Kyle chuckles, and I leave before the calm lightness subsides. You know, sometimes I think maybe I've been too hard on him all these years. I see Jeff and Julian and the strong bond that they have. I wonder what I have missed out on.

Kyle was just so damn arrogant and selfish when

he was younger. From day one, we have always been in competition. It went from who could build the tallest block tower to who could kiss our next door neighbor, Whitney, first. We've been this way our whole lives. But the thing I've always despised the most is his sense of entitlement. He thinks the world revolves around him, and I got sick of it.

He just used people around him for his own benefit, even if he had to destroy them in the process. I watched him single-handedly do this to many girls in the past, and I was the one that had to pick up the pieces with Mary, not him. At that point, I realized we had nothing in common but blood.

I see him with Maxine, though, and he's very different with her. She brought out a side of him that I never knew existed; it's refreshing to see. It makes me think that maybe at some point in the future my brother and I can have a relationship. For now, though, I just don't know how to move on from the past.

The rest of the day flies by, and it's now time to meet Jeff at the jewelers.

I have no idea why, but I'm nervous for him. This place is a little intimidating, but it's calming to see the excitement on the other men's faces and the couples in love. I'm a little envious.

I meet out front. "You ready?" I ask.

He looks as though he might pass out. I wonder if this has happened before. "Dude, I'm totally freaking!" he tells me honestly.

"Do you need to sit down a moment?"

He shakes his head. "No, let's do this!" he says loudly, trying to pump himself up.

I laugh. "Alright, man. Let's do this!"

After what seems like hours, Jeff has finally picked *the one*. He cashes out and takes the tiny little box with him. He looks proud until reality slams down on him.

"Dude, what if she says no?" He looks at me in complete freak mode.

I put my hands on his shoulders and look him straight in the eyes. "I don't know how you did it, but she loves you. There is no way she is saying no. You got this!" I tell him, trying to ease his worries.

He nods. "Yeah, she freaking loves me!"

"So when is this going down?"

Then his face consumes with fear and anxiety. "I don't know. I haven't gotten that far yet."

I can't help but laugh. "Okay, well if you need any help putting something together, just let me know. I'm here for you," I say to him.

"Thanks, bro. I appreciate it."

I leave him and head home. I look at my phone, and it's only seven thirty, which means Kinsey is probably home. I walk up to the apartment door and smell something amazing. My stomach immediately growls with hunger pains.

I enter the apartment and the first thing I notice is a clear walkway—no pumps to break my neck on. Then I see Kinsey in the kitchen, cooking away. She looks up and smiles; my heart flutters. She is *so* damn beautiful. How did I not notice this before?

"Hey, you hungry?" she asks. I look behind and around to make sure she's speaking to me. "Okay, jackass. Yes, I am talking to you," she informs me, rolling her eyes.

"Oh, well in that case, yes! I am starving!" I tell her, pulling out the stool to sit down at the kitchen counter. "What are you making?"

"Just some greens and beans with sausage. It's quick and easy to make. Did you stay at work late?" Kinsey asks as she washes off the escarole in the sink.

"Yeah, I had some things to take care of and a million emails to send out," I lie. "Do you want some wine?"

Kinsey breaks up the escarole and places it in the simmering pan. "Sure."

I choose a bottle of white to go with the dinner. I hold it up. "Relax?" I ask her, reading the label. She nods and puts the top on the pan for everything to cook.

I pour us both a glass and sit back on the barstool. Maybe this would be a good time to man up and talk about that kiss. "So listen, Kins—about that kiss—" I begin, but she stops me dead in my tracks.

"Junior, there's no need to discuss it. We are two adults that had a moment. It was nothing. Shit like this happens all the time. I've moved on from it, okay?" she clarifies. Of course it didn't feel like nothing to me. That kiss has affected these last couple of days completely, and she seemed to be affected by it for days after as well. So I don't believe a word she is saying right now.

"Wow, okay," I'm just gonna go with it. "If you're okay with it, then so am I."

Screw it. Why hash it out and ruin this dinner over a kiss?

"So let's not let it happen again," she adds. I agree.

I decide to take advantage of her openness. "What's with you and this Jax guy?" I pry.

She takes a sip of her wine. "We're just hanging; nothing serious yet. Why are you so interested?" she asks.

"He just seems a little player-ish if you ask me."

She stands across from me, taking another sip of her wine. Her eyebrows lift with my comment. "Really? I think your radar is a little off. I didn't get that vibe at all. I can usually sense bullshit a mile away."

She turns to stir the greens. "That smells delicious!"

"Thanks."

"But, if you ask me, I think you're wrong. Just be careful," I warn her.

She seems to take this into consideration. "So, when are you going to start dating?"

Damn, I don't know if I should tell her or not. "Well, actually—I took your advice. I'm having dinner with someone tomorrow."

She faces me, looking surprised. "Oh yeah? With anyone I know?"

"I asked Bridgette out."

She pauses for a moment, then turns to take the top off the food. "Bridgette, huh? I didn't see that one coming," she adds. She dishes out our plates. "Are you sure getting involved with someone we work with is such a good idea?"

She sounds like Maxine. "We kissed, and we got past it, right?" I'm not so sure this is the best question, but I also want to see her thoughts on us.

She contemplates this for a moment before responding. "Yes, but we have to face it; we live together, and we have close mutual friends together. You and Bridgette don't. So if things go bad, it could end up like Kyle and Beth," she explains.

I understand her concerns, but a little part of me is hoping her concerns may be for another reason—like not wanting anyone else to have me. Beth was our psycho coworker that Kyle hooked up with over a year ago. When he broke it off with her, she wouldn't take no for an answer, so my mother fired her.

Unfortunately, I feel like Kyle played a big part in that. If he wouldn't have lead her on the way he did, then maybe she would have gotten the point a lot earlier. I won't be doing this. I'm always upfront and honest.

"Let's just say I'm not Kyle, and she's not Beth. Unlike my brother, I handle women with respect and don't just throw them to the side when I'm finished," I say.

She squints her eyes and furrows her brows. "You know; I think you're more like your brother than you would like to admit. The way you just brushed me off after that kiss was just like Kyle's pre-Max self," she jabs right at my heart. Ouch.

"Aww! Come on Kins! I was out of it, and you were caught off guard, too, by my abruptness. But let's be honest—you were the one that pulled away from *me*! I didn't want to stop. Kissing you was fucking amazing! In fact, it's all that I think about! I want to jump over this counter and kiss you right now, but I'm afraid you will reject me," I admit, finally coming clean. I don't give a shit anymore. If I don't say it now, I may never say it, and then I will regret it.

She stands in front of me, speechless. Instead of speaking, she walks around the counter and rushes toward me. She grabs ahold of my face and brings me in for a jaw-dropping, spur-of-the-moment kiss. She's ruthless and sexy as hell. Even her abruptness is such a damn turn-on.

There's no hesitation or fear; this kiss is full of need and urgency, as though she has wanted this just as much as I have. The moment I glide my tongue deep into her mouth, she moans, and my dick rockets up. *Shit!* I'm in trouble.

I grab her hips, bringing her closer to me so she can *feel* just how much I want her. She leans her head back, allowing me to kiss down her neck while inhaling her erotic scent on the way down. She climbs on top of me, straddling me like a boss and begins to grind herself against my rock-hard bulge. I might just end up coming in my pants if she continues this motion.

I grab the hem of her tank top and rip it off over her head. God *damn!* She is completely bare—braless and magnificent, a beauty I have never witnessed before. I palm each breast in my hands, then lean down to take her hard, erect nipple into my mouth. Fuck, she is so hot! She immediately bucks up and grinds on me harder. This is dangerous. This is *very* dangerous.

I slide my hand down her stomach, under her sweatpants and into her panties. I just have to feel her. She catches her breath, then releases another soft moan after I stroke her swollen clit. She's dripping wet with need, and damn, it feels so good that this need is for me. I want to dip my tongue deep within her and taste every single last drop of her.

Kinsey lifts my shirt up over my head and runs her hands greedily down the front of me to the button on my jeans. "You look like a Greek god," she whispers. Our breathing is vigorous and erratic as we stare intensely into each other's eyes. Her eyes are begging for me to fuck her. How the hell did we get to this point? I don't know what it is about her, but she drives me completely mad. I've never wanted anyone in my entire life as much as I want her. I have this crazy magnetic pull toward her. What we're doing right now feels unbelievably right, but I know it's so wrong. In this moment, I couldn't care less, though. I'm allowing my dick to do the talking while my conscience is being pacified by those baby blues. But then guilt begins to consume me quickly.

I decide to stop her as she's unzipping my pants. I don't want to, but I also don't want her to have any regrets. She looks up at me with confusion. "I want you. I really do, but I think we should wait. Maybe we should just see where our friendship takes us, hangout together some more. I don't know how this happened, but I like you Kinsey, and I sure as hell can't stop thinking about you," I say to her, hoping she won't take this the wrong way.

She laughs—hard. "Are you serious, Junior? I'm here on top of you offering sex, not a date to the fucking prom."

I tilt my head to the side. "Wow, ok," I chuckle. I have to remember to take her with a grain of salt most of the time. "That was a little harsh, don't you think?"

She clicks her tongue, then hops off of me and grabs her shirt from the floor. I royally screwed up. These are the moments that I wish I was more like my brother and Jeff. "I'm sorry for being so blunt. What you see is what you get," she tells me, but I don't believe her one bit. "I've always known you're not like most men, because you've never once tried to get into my pants until now. I actually thought you might be stuck in the closet, but this is all confirmation that I was wrong. Of course you do have somewhat of a bitch trait."

What the fuck? Is she serious? "Wait, you thought I was gay?" I ask, laughing. "You've got to be kidding me! And what the fuck is a *bitch* trait?" I'm a little offended, but I'm comfortable with the man I am, so I'm not going to read into it too much, especially after this last mouth-to-body encounter. I think she's clear on my sexuality by now, but really, did she have to say that other stuff?

She walks back to the other side of the counter. "Okay, maybe I'm *exaggerating* a bit, but you sure had something up your ass; maybe it was just that damn stick," she taunts, then puts her hands up, surrendering after seeing my face. "That was a joke. I swear," she declares, still laughing. "And yes, a bitch trait. You know, you have emotions and a conscience more like a girl than a man about to get his dick wet," she spits out. I just shake my head. I still can't get used to her vulgar mouth. I like it better when my tongue is in it.

"Thanks, asshole. But let's keep that title under wraps," I tell her. If the guys ever heard that one, they would never let me live it down. Man, she is something else. What the hell am I going to do with her? Just days ago, I would have come through the door and walked straight to my room. I would have never entertained the idea of eating dinner with her, but now, I'm actually enjoying the little banter we have going back and forth.

She can be crass at times, but I think she's growing on me. Structure and routine is something I've become accustomed to in my life, but she's beginning to open my eyes. Up until now, I've always played life safe. I don't know how, but she brings color to my gray, drab world.

I smirk and shake my head. "I might be kicking myself in the ass later for this one, but how about Wednesday I cook us some dinner and we can hang out here?" I suggest.

She finishes her bite of greens and beans. "Yeah, I'm cool with that. Jax is taking me out on Saturday, so that won't be an issue."

My gut sinks. Oh yeah—Jax. "Okay, yeah. Cool," I respond, putting a huge bite of food into my mouth so I won't be able to speak for a moment.

"Will you be meeting Bridgette here tomorrow?" she asks.

I shake my head. "No, we're meeting at the bar after work," I answer.

"That new bar, The Tavern?"

Hmm ... is someone getting a little jealous? I think

I'm liking this side of her. "Yup, that's the one."

"I liked that place. McGregor's is old news. I'm retiring that place to those hoe bags in Beth's crew," she snarls.

I almost spit out my wine at that comment. "Kins, you are out of control. You know that?"

She rolls her eyes. "You're just now noticing this?" she questions sarcastically. "So tell me something, Romeo —I didn't take you for a serial dater. You said you never dated unless you saw potential for the future?"

"Well, I thought about what you said when we went out for lunch last week. You sort of opened my eyes a bit. It's time I start broadening my horizons and get out in the dating world," I inform her.

She takes sip of her wine. "Huh, okay, well I'm glad my words made an impact on you, but just so we're clear—what are we doing exactly?"

"Hanging out?"

She taps her fingers on her mouth. "And does this 'hanging' include kissing and touching?"

"I don't see why not," I add, shrugging my

shoulders.

She furrows her brows. "And will you be kissing and touching others?"

"Will you?" I turn the question back on her. Normally, I'm not into being romantic with more than one person, but if she can do it, why can't I?

"*Well*—I'm not really sure. I've never had rules to 'hanging' before. Usually no one makes it past the first date with me!"

I chuckle. "Yes, I heard. Kyle told me what happened to that poor guy before Jax."

She looks shocked. "Umm, first of all, he was not a *poor guy*, and second of all, he deserved every last bit of my wrath for being such a douche!"

This time it's me putting my hands up, surrendering. "Okay, okay, I got it. He deserved it!" I can't stop laughing. This is such a change for me. I can't remember the last time I laughed this hard.

"Okay, since we almost just fucked—do me a favor —if you get in that position with anyone else, let me go. I don't want to be friends with benefits if you're screwing anyone else," she states so bluntly.

"Agreed."

"Good, now that we've gotten that settled, I'm going to take a shower and hit the sack. Mondays always exhaust me. I cooked; you clean," Kinsey says.

I watch her walk off as I shake my head. There are so many things running through my mind right now. She can be annoying and sarcastic as hell, but what I'm picking up is that it's just a protective shield. I saw the signs before, but now I am sure of it. I want to know why though. Who caused her pain? Because honestly—I want to be the one to fix it.

In only just a couple of days she has cracked my walls, and I'm beginning to see the tiny rays of light seeping through. It has me blindsided and a little uneasy, but on the other hand, the feeling I have when her lips touch mine is electrifying. How can I ignore the obvious? I know I may be playing with fire, but I'm sick of always being cold. If I don't take risks now, I will forever be alone.

CHAPTER SIX

Kinsey

Yup. I have completely lost it. I just mounted Junior like a rabid cat in heat and then agreed to a possible friends-with-benefits situation. How the freak did this happen? No more drinking wine with him. Wine and Junior equals really, really bad decisions.

I jump into the steamy, hot shower, letting the water hit my neck and shoulders. Work was a little stressful today. Max had me working like a dog. I think I should use some vacation time to go down to South Carolina to visit my parents. I could use some warm breeze against my skin and some sand between my toes.

My mother and I are very close. I talk to her at least once a day. She was my rock growing up. If it wasn't for her by my side during my extremely tough year, I don't know what I would have done.

I was in tenth grade when it all happened. The lead singer, Tommy, from one of the local bands was a senior in my high school. I never paid much attention to him; I didn't really care what he was about. I really wasn't a fan of his music, either, and he always had groupies following him like he was a god or something—completely annoying.

I had my pick of boys in that school; I was popular and well-liked, but I was sick of dating the jocks and muscle heads. They were just into hooking up and partying; there wasn't too much depth to them. That shit got boring. I was into getting good grades so I could make something of myself. I always had goals and a path that I followed, even at a young age. But Tommy almost ruined that all for me.

My girlfriend begged me to go to a party with her. I hated these sort of things, but Tommy's band was playing that night and she really wanted to go, so I agreed. That was the biggest mistake of my life.

It was late, and the band just got done playing. I needed to get some air. The party was jam-packed, and I was feeling claustrophobic, so I went out back. I saw Tommy sneaking out to do the same. He saw me sitting by myself while lighting up a cigarette. I was secretly pleading for him not to come over, but he did.

To my surprise, he was sweet and charming: everything I thought he wouldn't be. After we talked that night, he made an effort to find me every day at school until he knew my schedule by heart. At first, I tried brushing him off, would show little interest, and maybe played a little hard to get. But he grew on me, and over the next couple of weeks, he tore my guard down. I couldn't believe that I had actually fallen in love with this town icon, this boy that every girl threw themselves at. He wanted me.

After months of being with him, I decided I was ready to give him my virginity. This was going to be a monumental step with someone I loved and trusted—at least I thought. The day after, he wouldn't return my calls. He stopped coming by my locker at school and walking me to my classes. When I finally saw him, he was holding hands with another girl. I was devastated and completely heartbroken, but that wasn't the worst part.

After crying myself to sleep every night, I came in one Monday morning and was the laughing stock of the school. He videotaped our night together in his bedroom and showed it off to everyone and anyone who wanted to watch it. I was more than mortified, and I had thoughts of suicide for the first time ever.

My parents knew something was off, but how the hell was I supposed to tell them their daughter was a whore? It was my best friend that had to come clean to them, and honestly, I never once felt betrayed by her. She was worried and had every right to be.

My parents hired a lawyer, and Tommy ended up expelled for the act, but his life went on. He got his GED and went on with his music career as if nothing happened. I, on the other hand, was constantly bullied and reminded everyday how much of an easy skank I was. I was afraid to leave my house. I went into a deep depression that would have killed me.

My mother made the final decision to close her store so we could move. She changed her whole life so I could have a new one, and she did it without a thought in the world. We moved, and I built myself back up again, but I have never, *ever* allowed myself to be in that position again. I love sex, but I love it on my own terms, without feeling or commitment. I won't allow myself to slip again, even if my heart is screaming for it.

So this is why I am the way I am.

I get out and dry myself off. I pull the towel tight around me and then laugh at myself for it. Junior has already manhandled my chest and had his fingers all over my goodies, so I guess it's a little silly now to be concerned about keeping my towel together.

After doing my nightly hygiene routine, I hop into bed and let the night take me away.

The morning goes by smoothly. To my surprise, there's no awkward silence between us in the kitchen as we gather the coffee I set the night before. I crack a couple of comments, and he just shakes his head like normal. I love shocking him and throwing him off. I'm sick; I kind of get a kick out of seeing him squirm.

Junior's always so rigid and uptight. Sometimes I just want to shake him or punch him in the gut for some other type of reaction, but I'm not sure that would go over too well. I'll keep it friendly and light so I don't push him over the edge. Although, I wonder what might happen if I did? Sick, I know. I can't help it.

I get to work, and I've only had my second cup of coffee before I'm thrown into all-day meetings with Max. That vacation idea is looking more and more appealing as the day goes on. I follow Max into her office after the meeting and plop down dramatically in the chair in front of her desk.

"God, I really hope the rest of the week isn't like today," I comment.

Max snorts. "Yeah, you and I both."

"So listen, I'm gonna need some time off."

Her head snaps up from her computer. "Why? What's going on?"

"I'm going to go visit the parents for a week. You know how Mom is; she keeps stalking me about coming home. Honestly, though, I could use the relaxation time. These past couple of months have been brutal on us," I tell her.

She nods. "Yes, you're right on that. Since I've merged our companies, we've taken on a lot of new clients. But I think you're doing great, Kins." I was with Max when she first opened up her own literary agency. I helped her build it from the ground up as her assistant—her backbone. So last year when she made the decision to grow and expand her agency by merging her company with Saunders Literary Agency, I was right there with her. "Have you thought about moving up to an agent?" Max asks.

"I'm not too sure. Maybe in the future. Actually, I've been thinking about doing some writing of my own," I admit. I majored in English Literature, because of my love for books. I've always had a love for writing, just never had the time to do it. Lately, I've been getting the urge or calling, if you will, to let my fingers flow. I've just been too pussy to do it. I'm afraid of failure. What if I suck? And what the hell am I going to even write about, let alone in what genre?

"No way! Really, Kins? That's great. What are you waiting for?" she asks.

I shrug. "I don't know where to begin."

Max looks me head-on. "You do what you've been telling other authors for years. You sit your ass down and just write—anything and everything until you finish. You know I would support anything you decide, right?"

My heart pings with love. "Thanks, Max. That means a lot. Maybe I'll start once I'm back home and my mind is clear."

"Ok, this week? Next week?" she asks.

"I'm thinking about taking off next weekend. You sure you don't want to come with? I'm sure your brothers would love to see you." I try my hardest to sucker her in. Maybe make a girls trip out of it.

"Actually, Luke is coming next month for a week. He's dying to see Penelope. He hasn't seen her since she was first born. Oh, I think I forgot to tell you, Justin and Valerie have set a date for their wedding: July of this summer! So look out for the invitation; I gave him your address," she tells me.

"No shit! Wow, I never thought his wild ass would be settling down. He loved them girls, and the girls sure did love them some Justin!" I say with a laugh.

"Boy, you are so right. That kid had them lined up at the door. Luke had to scare them away, but considering what we came from, somehow Justin turned out to be a really good man. We both have Luke to thank for our lives now," she says sadly.

"And what about yours and Kyle's wedding date?" I question.

She shakes her head and huffs. "I don't know. Soon I guess. I'm just too busy with work and Penelope!" I get that. It's hard to think about planning a wedding with everything she has going on right now.

I get up and walk around her desk to give her a big, supportive hug. "I know, babe. You guys will figure it out, and Luke *is* an amazing guy. Speaking of the past—have you heard from your father lately?" I know I'm dipping into Pandora's Box with this topic.

She groans. "Ugh! He calls at least once a week. I just ignore the call and throw his ass to voicemail. I stopped listening to his messages a long time ago, though. Everything he said was for his benefit, not out of love. He has no remorse for what he has done, but now that he's engaged to be married again, he decides he needs his kids around so he doesn't look like such a loser father to his fiancé and her family. I'm not with that," she explains.

"What a fucking douche! You know my parents are there for you anytime you need them, right? They love you and think of you as another daughter. So don't ever think you're alone."

"I know, Kins. Your family is the best. Ok, so I'm putting your vacation time in now. I'll let Connie know also, so no worries."

I leave Max's office to head to mine. I pass Junior's office on the way and see Bridgette sitting in there. She's giggling like a little schoolgirl, which totally turns my stomach. Junior looks up, watching me pass. I disconnect and look away. I can only imagine what will be going down on their date tonight. He's been pretty hands on with me these last couple of days, when he swears up and down that it is out of character for him. I just don't want to think about his hands being on anyone else. The thought completely irks me.

It's finally five o'clock and time to clock out. My

phone dings, notifying me of a text—it's Jax. I smile.

"Hey there, pretty. I have some free time tonight. Do you want to grab some dinner and drinks somewhere?" he asks.

Hmm, I think he may have just saved me from a night of sulking. "Sure. When and where?" I text back.

"I'll come pick you up in an hour," he responds.

"K."

I think my night is most definitely looking up. Now my goal is to get Junior the fuck out of my head! Just a couple of hours is all I need. It's enough time to give Jax a moment to shine. Let's be real, though—neither of them will be penetrating my heart. I've learned my lesson. I won't make the same mistake twice.

Let's not get things twisted. I may be thinking about Junior, but that doesn't mean I'm going to fall in love with him after I fuck him. It's sexual tension and that's it, plain and simple. We may go a couple of rounds, but after that, I'll move on to the next.

Men have been doing this for years, so why can't I?

I'm not promiscuous by any means, I'm actually quite the opposite. I'm picky as hell until someone makes my panties wet, and then it's game on for me. I like the chase; it can be a great form of foreplay. But once the excitement and fun fizzles out and commitment is mentioned—I'm out. I don't look back.

I freshen up a bit before Jax arrives. I buzz him in from the intercom, and when he comes through the door, he looks around. When he doesn't see Junior in sight, he relaxes just a bit.

"Hey there," he says, giving me a kiss on the cheek. "Where's your roommate?" he wonders.

"He's actually out on a date as we speak," I inform him.

He smiles and then grabs me, pulling me into him. Before I can say another word, he brings me in for a deep, passionate kiss. I'll give it to him; he's good. He knows just the right moves at just the right moments.

I try to pull back just a bit, but he holds onto me just a bit tighter. I'm feeling a bit claustrophobic, and I need some air. I pull my lips away from him, and he begins kissing down my neck. "I've missed you," he whispers between kisses. Oh no, we're not doing this already! Red flag!

I place my hands on his chest as I did before to push him back a bit. He gets the point and releases me. "Are you ready?" he asks.

"Yes," I say with relief.

We head out to his SUV and get on our way. He takes a left onto Lake Avenue, heading to the outskirts of downtown. Moments later, we pull into a parking lot, and I know just where we are—The Tavern. Shit. This is not good.

"We're going *here*?" I ask, a little taken aback. I know Junior will be in here with Bridgette. My guts sinks. A part of me wants to tell him to turn around, but another small part of me wants to see. Are they laughing? Are they flirting? Is he looking at her the same way he looks at me? Ugh! What the fuck is *wrong* with me?

"Yeah, I know the bartender, Jessica, pretty well," he answers. "She makes the best drinks."

He parks. I see Junior's car parked diagonal from

us. My stomach is now full of those pesky, nervous butterflies. "Oh yeah?"

"I actually used to date her sister a couple years back," he tells me. I take this little piece of information in and store it for another time—interesting. "Do you still see the sister?"

We head up towards the door. "Every now and then I see her in court. We dated back in law school," he explains while holding the door open for me. I hand over my ID to the bouncer at the door.

My eyes dart around as soon as I walk in until they land on exactly what I'm looking for—Junior and Bridgette sitting at a secluded table in the back corner. A flame of fire spreads throughout my body with fury, making my blood boil. It's one thing to know he's on a date, but it's another thing to actually *see* it. I feel a tiny bit of jealousy creep up on me, and I absolutely hate the feeling. I avoid getting close to anyone, because I don't want to feel, and here I go completely betraying my own self.

They look like they're enjoying each other's company. Junior doesn't look tense or annoyed. Just as I'm about to look away, he looks up, and his eyes connect with mine. He looks confused, and I see a scowl on his face when his eyes land on Jax. Good. I smile within, knowing I just caused that face.

I link my arm with Jax's as we head to the bar, and I put a little more oomph in my step. I feel the hole being burned into my back as Junior glares after me.

The chick behind the bar squeals when she notices Jax. I think she just blew my eardrum out. She leans over the bar—with her very low T-shirt, might I add—and wraps him up in her arms for a hug. Geez, is he sure he didn't date this sister as well?

"Oh my God, Jax! It's so good to see you again! Did you come here to see me?" she questions with a flirty twinkle in her eye. Yup, she's got it bad for him. Bitch better step off of him before I remove her myself.

He clears his throat and then looks to me. "Actually, I'm having some drinks with a friend."

She smiles while giving me a once-over. "What can I get you both?" Her spirit's been crushed. Poor girl had high hopes that he was actually here for her.

"I'll take a Cosmopolitan," I tell her.

She then looks to Jax. "Jack on the rocks?" he nods and pulls out his barstool to sit. Does he really think that I want to sit here and stare at her all night?

Jax looks over to me, and he must notice the sour look on my face. "Would you rather sit in a booth?" he questions. Duh, dimwit!

"Sure, a booth sounds nice," I tell him, biting my tongue. We take our drinks and sit in a booth across the room from Junior, but it's still not far enough.

"Hey, isn't that your roommate?" Jax asks.

"Yes."

"Should we go over and say hi?" he questions. The waitress comes over to see if we're going to need a menu. Then Jax tells her to bring Junior and his date a round of drinks, on him.

You know what? I think that's exactly what we need to do. "Yes, let's go over."

I jump out of my seat, maybe a little too excitedly, and strut right over to Junior's table. He looks up, not surprised at all. He already knows my bold moves all too well. "Well hello, you two," I smirk evilly.

Jax walks around me to slap Junior up, and Bridgette smiles at me, completely clueless that I almost fucked her date the other night.

"So, what brings you two here?" Junior asks, eyeing the both of us.

"Jax here knows the bartender," I answer just a little too quickly. Junior looks behind him to get a glance at the bartender and then looks back to me. I know that look. He already thinks Jax is a player, and I'm sure this just added to his theory.

"Oh yeah?" Junior adds. "Did you guys used to date?" he asks Jax.

I roll my eyes. Did he really have to go there? He's such an ass!

Jax laughs. "No, we definitely did not."

The waitress comes over with their drinks, and Junior thanks Jax, clearly annoyed.

"So, Bridgette—how's Jonathan doing?" I ask. Her face turns a light shade of pink. They can't start a relationship on a lie, now can they?

Jonathan is another agent who had the biggest crush on Maxine when she first moved here, but of course Max tried her hardest to play matchmaker to the two of us. Jonathan is a nice guy, but he just wasn't the right guy for me. I would have chewed him up and spit him out for breakfast.

It's been known at work that Jonathan and Bridgette have been seeing each other; I'm just not sure Junior pays close enough attention to these sort of things. He probably wouldn't have asked her out if he knew.

Junior's brows furrow with confusion. "He's good —I think. We haven't spoken in a little while, though," Bridgette responds, clearly avoiding Junior's face.

Junior jumps in. "Jonathan? Are the two of you dating?"

I just dropped the grenade, now it's time for me to leave before it blows up in my face. "Hey, listen, it was nice seeing you guys. Jax and I are going to go order some food."

Neither of them say a word. Jax and I sneak off.

"Wow, that was a little intense," Jax comments.

I stare back over to Junior's table where I left my thoughts. Jax is just background noise at the moment. He finally waves his hands in front of me to get my attention. I shake my thoughts off. "Yeah, I probably should have mentioned Jonathan to Junior when he told me about their date, but I figured he knew," I lie, shrugging my shoulders.

I look over the menu, trying to concentrate on something else other than Junior, but it's really hard, because they look to be having a pretty intense conversation—and it's all my fault.

"So, tell me, did you and Junior ever have a thing?"

Shit! Am I making it that obvious? "No, why?"

The waitress comes over with another round of drinks. Jax looks up toward Jessica and nods his head with a huge grin to thank her. We order our food. "It's just the way he looks at you when you're not looking," he explains.

Hmm, that's a new one. "No, he's actually like an annoying little brother that I never wanted," I answer. This part is true, at least.

"Well I don't think that's how he sees it. Looks like

I may have some competition," Jax says. Geez, if he only knew. "How long have you been roomies?"

I take a sip of my Cosmo. "Umm, around eight months or so. I originally got the apartment with Max, but then her and Kyle moved in together. I needed a roommate, and Junior's place was going up for sale. So this was a quick fix until my lease is up in about three months. I may just buy a small house after, instead of renting."

Jax nods. "So how do the sleeping arrangements work?"

Is he serious? What the fuck kind of question is this? "Oh, we sleep in the same bed. We just don't fuck," I respond sarcastically. He's got me aggravated now.

He chuckles. "Okay, okay, I deserved that. I'm sorry; I have a little jealousy streak that I need to learn how to control. I've never dated a woman that lived with another man. This is all new to me, so you'll have to be patient with me," he informs me. I can understand this, and unfortunately, his radar is dead-on about Junior and me.

"I get it, but I'm not with the side comments. If you don't want a fucked up answer, then don't ask me a fucked up question," I warn.

"Fair enough."

The waitress finally comes over with our food. I ordered the loaded nachos, and he ordered chicken quesadillas so we could share. I look over to Junior and Bridgette's table, and they have left. How the hell did I not see this? They just snuck right out. I didn't even get to see if they left on good terms or not.

We finish our food while making small talk over another round of drinks. He wanted to come up when he dropped me off, but I've had enough for the night. We say our goodbyes in the car, and I head up to my apartment by myself. Junior's car was not parked in the garage. It's now my turn to wait up for him.

CHAPTER SEVEN

Junior

Man, tonight was a weird one—definitely not how I hoped it would pan out. I was praying that Bridgette might take my mind off of Kinsey, but of course, it had the opposite affect once Kinsey showed up with Jax.

Bridgette is a pretty cool chick. I would have never asked her out if I knew she had something going on with Jonathan. She explained their situation to me and assured me they were no longer dating. The whole thing still makes me uncomfortable, but everyone has an ex, so I can't really hold that against her.

I walked her out to her car and went in for the kiss. I'm usually not this bold, but I needed to know if this thing with Kinsey is real or not. I was actually hoping something would spark with Bridgette just so I could write Kinsey off as freak accident, but the damn kiss did nothing for me. Not even a flutter in my dick. Now what am I supposed to do?

Bridgette and I made plans to see a movie this weekend, but I'm worried about leading her on. I refuse to be my brother. I just might have to cancel and add her to the friend zone. Maybe I can just explain that it's me, not her. I shake my head. Yeah, right. I would be an idiot to use that line.

It's now nine o'clock. I went for a long drive to clear my head. Honestly, I didn't want to look like a loser by getting home before Kinsey. I just want her to know that her little interrogation with Bridgette didn't work like she was probably hoping it would. Of course, that would mean she cared, and I just can't tell with her. She can be so hot and then so ice cold at times.

I enter the apartment expecting shoes to be sprawled around, but I get nothing. Kinsey's shoes are nicely lined up next to the door where they should be, which means she's home. The living room TV is on, but I don't see her anywhere. I walk over to the couch, and she's curled up, sleeping like a little baby.

I turn off the TV and lift her in my arms to take her

to her bed. She wraps her arms around me and nuzzles into my neck. My dick gets hard automatically. God, how the hell does she *do* this?

Her hair smells of blossoms and melon. I know the exact shampoo she uses. Living with a girl, you start to recognize the products that she uses. Not by choice but by default.

Walking into her room, I almost trip on a million things. She has clothes spread over her bed and chair, shoes strewn all over the floor, and junk all over her make-up stand and dressers. It looks like a tornado hit. How the hell does she live in all this chaos?

I move the clothes over and lay her down onto her bed. When I try to remove her hands from around my neck, she holds on tighter, bringing me down to her level. I can't tell if she is dreaming or if she's awake, so I try lightly to pull her hands from my neck again.

"Don't go. Kiss me, please?" she begs with a whisper.

"Kins, you're tired. Go to bed," I tell her. Man, the last thing I want to do is leave.

Her eyes open and she stares at me so openly that I feel as though I can almost read her mind. She wants me just as much as I want her. I lean down and immediately smash my lips against hers. I have no more control. All rationality is lost. I am prisoner to her in every way possible, and I am completely okay with it.

Her lips are so velvety soft and perfect; I feel as though I'm in heaven. She opens her mouth, slightly allowing my tongue to slip in and tangle with hers. A light moan releases from her, going straight to my cock. Damn, I am in some big trouble.

She pulls me on top of her, then turns me over so she is the one straddled on top of me. How the hell? I didn't even see this coming. She's wearing only her tiny, white cotton tank top and boxers, leaving almost nothing to the imagination.

She leans down to kiss me, and when she pulls away, she has my bottom lip between her teeth. She begins to grind slowly over my rock-hard bulge. It's begging to be freed, and if she continues like this, I won't last too long. I'm overly aroused, and it's been too long since I've been with a woman, let alone a smoking hot one that belongs on a *Playboy* cover.

"Damn, Kins, what are you doing to me?" I ask between kisses.

She leans over to my ear and whispers, "Do you have a condom on you?"

My heart picks up a million more beats per minute with excitement. Just the other night, I was trying to stop this to keep myself in check, but I just don't have the strength any longer. I want her. I want every single inch of her. I want to be nuzzled deep inside of her.

"No, but I have one in my room," I tell her.

She reaches over to her nightstand and opens the drawer. She hands me a gold-wrapped condom and slides down my legs enough to reach for my zipper. I grab her hand to stop her for a moment. "Hey, what's the rush? We have all night."

"I want your dick inside of me now. I don't want to wait," she says with a pout. How can I resist that?

"Okay."

She unzips my zipper and reaches into my pants to

release my rock-hard dick from the confines of my clothing. Her eyes grow wide, then she looks up to me. "Damn, Junior."

I chuckle and then lift my ass up so she can yank my pants off. Her nipples are ripping through the thin cotton, dying to be set free, so I reach for the hem of her tank and pull it up over her head. God, she's gorgeous. I reach for her and tangle my fingers through her hair to bring her down to me. Our lips connect and all doubt and nervousness fly out of the window. I'm ready to ravage this beauty like a hungry beast.

I move from her lips to place tiny kisses along her jawline and down her neck to her breasts. I take her nipple into my mouth, sucking slowly and lightly; grazing my teeth against her skin. She moans loudly while arching her back, enjoying every moment of this. She's going to make me cum before she even sinks down on it.

She grabs a hold of my throbbing dick, and I hiss through my teeth as she strokes me up and down with her hands. I tug at her shorts, and she lifts herself enough for me to rip them off. I never imagined a naked body could ever be so damn perfect, but hers is—perfectly perfect.

I rip open the condom wrapper with my teeth and roll it over myself. She shifts her body so she is hovering over me; the entrance of her pussy now touching the tip of my dick. I love the fact that she is trimmed nicely but not bare. It's such a fucking turn-on.

"Are you ready?" she asks.

"Are *you*?" I ask back.

She slowly sinks down on me. My whole body locks up as the feel of her takes over every inch of me. She's so warm and tight; we fit so perfectly. I wish that just for a moment I wasn't wearing this condom and could feel her against my skin.

"Damn, you feel amazing," I tell her.

I grab a hold of her hips tightly while she begins to ride me like a cowgirl. Damn, she feels so fucking good. I have to close my eyes to concentrate so I don't blow a gasket yet. Every thrust and every movement hits me right down to the core. She leans over me, crashing her lips against mine. She tastes so fucking good. I can't wait to taste her arousal. After this, I'm getting her into the shower so we can do this all over again.

She sits up with her palms against my chest, breast bare, nipples taunt, and grinds on me wildly. She's driving me out of my mind. A wave of heat crashes over me, and I'm completely helpless as I groan out loud. I feel her insides begin to convulse around me, and I know she is right behind me. Just the sound of my name rolling off her tongue pushes me over the edge, and we tumble down an orgasmic mountain together.

She falls down on top of me to catch her breath. We sound as though we just ran a 5K in under ten minutes. I run my fingers up and down her spin, then kiss her temple. She clams up, then pushes off of me to get her clothes.

I sit up, confused. "Where are you going?" I question, brows furrowed.

She looks at me like I'm crazy. "Junior, we just fucked. I don't do the cuddling thing. I'm tired and ready for bed. Do you mind?"

Is she fucking serious? "I don't understand why you're acting like this. Did I do something wrong?" I ask.

She puts her tank top and boxers back on, then grabs my clothes and hands them to me. "No, Junior. You did everything right. I'm just not into all the extra stuff, okay? It's just the way I am."

My whole body fires up with anger. I've never been so pissed in my life. She's treating me like I'm some fucking booty call. How the hell did I let this happen? "Why? Why are you being like this, Kinsey?"

I stand up and put my boxers on, waiting for her to respond. "I don't know, Junior. I am who I am. My past experiences have made me the way I am today. No offense, but I'm just not interested in something serious. Cuddling leads to feelings, and feelings allow you to get burned. Like I said before—I'm cool with hanging out as friends and even fucking, but the rest of it—leave it for someone who wants it. Bridgette is your best bet," she divulges.

I shake my head, running my hand through my hair. I am completely perplexed on how this even happened, right down to the kissing and sex. "Bridgette and I are better off as friends, but if this is how you want it to be, I guess I have no choice but to respect your wishes. I'm going to turn in now. Goodnight," I tell her.

At this point, I'm not even pissed. I feel a bit lost and even sad for her. Whatever happened in her past must have really fucked her up to shape her this way; she can't even be affectionate without having a total meltdown. I don't know if I can stay away from her. I don't know when or how it became apparent, but I have feelings for her. After tonight, it's clear as day for me. I'm not going to give up. Somehow I'm going to make her see this as well.

My eyes feel like sandpaper, rough and burning from lack of sleep. I tossed and turned all damn night, thinking of Kinsey: her lips, her touch, and the warmth of her body against mine—in and out.

I drag my ass to the bathroom to take a nice, hot shower. It wakes me up, revives my energy. I'm going to need it to get through the day. We have a long, detailed meeting to deal with this afternoon. It's one of our agent monthly meetings that my dad throws together to get us all on the same page. We go over our clients in detail as well as any new ideas that could help the agency. Things change in this business every day, so there's a constant demand to keep up.

I finish getting dressed and head out to the kitchen to get some coffee. I hear Kinsey's heels clicking around in there. Whelp, I gotta face her. It's now or never. We're two grown adults that had sex—I can do this.

I turn the corner, and there she is, fucking hot as hell. I clear my throat. "Good morning," I say to her, walking to the cupboard to grab a coffee mug.

She stiffens for a brief second, then relaxes. "Good morning to you. How did you sleep?" she asks.

I almost feel as though she's taunting me. "Like crap," I spit out honestly. Why sugarcoat it?

Her brows furrow. "Oh, I thought after last night you would have slept great."

Is she out of her mind right now? I know it's early in the morning, but what the hell is wrong with this chick?

I finish mixing my coffee and walk around the counter to take a seat on the barstool. "Well, you thought wrong. Are we still on for tonight, or will it be too much for you?"

She smirks at me with a mischievous twinkle in her eyes. "Is that a challenge, Mr. Saunders? Because I'm all up for challenges as long as you don't get your panties in a bunch when I send you packing," she teases.

"Oh, now you got jokes, huh?"

Kinsey prances over toward me. My heart begins to pick up, and my palms get a little sweaty. Just something about her makes my blood pump through my veins vigorously. She stands in between my legs, looking sexy as hell for eight in the morning with her blue fuck-me pumps. "Don't get yourself involved with something you can't handle," I warn her.

She begins to unzip my pants, but I immediately place my hand over hers. "We have to be to work in thirty minutes," I remind her, right eyebrow arched.

She hikes up her skirt, then drops her panties while standing in front of me with a come-hither look. My dick gets hard immediately. Two can play this game. I stand up, lift her off her feet, and set her down on the counter. I unzip my pants and drop them, then grab my cock and hold it at her entrance. "Is this what you want?"

"Yes," she responds all breathy. Who *am* I? I don't ever say these things. She just brings out the animal in me, and I fucking love it.

I slam myself deep into her. She yells out in pure pleasure. I continue to pump into her, hard and deep, until her nails dig into my shoulders through my shirt.

"Fuck, yes!" she screams. I'm not going to last much longer with her screaming and moaning in my ear while her warm pussy convulses around my cock. I give her one last pump that sets us both over the edge, then quickly pull out so I don't end up coming inside of her. That would not be a smart move. I'm not even sure if I asked if she's on birth control. Shit! I'm never this careless.

"Are you on birth control?" I ask while grabbing her a paper towel to clean up.

She lifts her one eyebrow. "You're asking me this question *now*?"

I chuckle. "Yeah, I guess I am."

"Yes, I am on birth control."

I hand her the paper towel. "And you've been

checked out? You're clean?" she asks me.

"And you're asking *this* now?" I tease back.

She rolls her eyes. "I know, you caught me off guard. I didn't think you were going to make this move," she admits.

"Oh yeah?"

"Yeah," she says while putting her panties back on.

I zip my pants back up and tuck in my button-up shirt. "Yes, I have been checked, and I have a clean bill of health. You?"

"Yes, I am good to go," she replies.

I grab my car keys after putting my coffee mug in the sink. Damn, I feel like a million bucks right now! "Do you want to ride together? We can stop and get some takeout before we head home—"

She thinks about my offer for a moment. "Yeah, okay. I'm okay with that."

I hold back a smile.

CHAPTER EIGHT

Kinsey

Damn, I needed that. I never knew Junior had it in him, but damn, when he lets go—he lets *go*! As long as he understands that what we have going on isn't going to turn into anything serious, then I think this little agreement just might work to both of our benefits. I can date whomever I want with no pressure on the sexual needs and come home to Junior when I'm horny and ready to get fucked. I just hope he does the same.

We showed up to work together a little late. Bridgette was on high alert when she saw Junior and I walking in together. I have to admit, I got a little pleasure out of that, and as soon as I left his side, she went running into his office. The best part about this whole thing is that his dick is covered in my juices.

I'm not even in my office for five minutes before Max walks in. She leans against the doorjamb. "Hey, Kins. So what's the deal? I don't think you've been a day late since you started working for me," she comments, looking at me a little closer. "Whoa! You are freaking glowing! What have *you* been doing Miss Balterson?"

I swear, I can never get anything past her. "Close the door and take a seat," I instruct.

Max lights up. She does exactly what I ask. "Okay, come on! Spill it!" she demands as she sits down.

"Okay, brace yourself," I tell her. She huffs, clearly annoyed. "I slept with Junior last night and this morning," I reveal.

Her jaw drops before she can even gather a sentence together. "Okay, holy shit! Was it good?"

My smile radiates before I even answer. "*So* fucking good! Mr. Rigid and Boring actually knows how to let go some. Who would have ever thought?"

"What the hell happened to Jax?" Max asks. Oh yeah—Jax.

"Umm, we're still talking, but nothing serious. Junior and I just kind of happened. But I was very clear with him that this is all it will ever be—friends with benefits."

Max bursts out laughing. "Kins, you are too freaking much! And Junior was actually okay with all of this?"

"Well, he was a little bent out of shape last night when I told him to go into his own bed, but this morning, in the kitchen, I think he felt a little better about the decision," I tell her while brushing my shoulder off.

"You know Bridgette has been telling people that her and Junior went out last night, right?" Max informs.

I roll my eyes. "Really? She's already opening her mouth? She probably is hoping shit might get back to Jonathan."

"That's exactly what I was thinking, too! I told Junior she wasn't right for him, but I guess he's gotta get burned to learn," Max comments.

My phone vibrates. It's a text from Jax. I hold the phone up. "Jax," I tell Max.

Her eyes bug out. She is absolutely loving this. She gets a little stir crazy being home with a baby when she's not working. "What's it say?"

"He's just asking what movie I want to see this

weekend. And by the way, Junior said he's not interested in Bridgette that way," I advise her.

I text Jax back, and he wants to pick me up Saturday, because he has something special planned after the movie. I have to admit this makes me a little nervous. I hope it's not a plan in which he thinks he might get laid, because there is no way I am sleeping with two men in the same week. That's just not my style.

"Well of course he isn't, because his eyes are on you. I told you he had a *thing* for you. I think Bridgette was someone to just occupy his time until you figured out you also have a *thing* for him," Max suggests. Oh, she's being funny now, huh?

I squint my eyes in her direction, daring her to say another word. She holds her hands up in defense. "Okay, okay. I'm going now," she says as she gets up from the chair and turns back around to me. "Oh, we've moved the meeting up to eleven, so don't be late. Bring the folders for each client we are working with. Also, Mr. Saunders is on his shit today, so expect his crass bluntness," she warns, and thankfully so. It's good to know what I'm walking into.

Finally, the meeting has broke for lunch. It's only been two hours, and my head is completely spinning. Elise and I decided to grab something from the small diner down the street, but before we go, I need to check up on my staff.

I grab Shane, my go-to guy, and pull him aside.

"What's happening on the floor? Why does everyone look so agitated?" I ask.

He looks as though he doesn't want to spill the beans, but I give him "the look," and he's helpless. "I guess Beth is outside, waiting for Matt right now. Some of the girls saw her out there, and then they saw Kyle coming out of the meeting—" he explains.

This bitch just doesn't know how to stay away. I got something for her little ass. "Thanks for the info, Shane. Tell everyone to calm down and get back to work," I instruct.

I go into my office, grab my purse and keys, and head out to the parking lot with a vengeance. I'll be damned if Max sees her outside. Beth's not getting anywhere near my girl!

I push the security door open, and I can immediately see Beth sitting in the driver's seat through the glass doors ahead. It's clear she wants to be the first thing anyone sees when they walk out. I'm assuming she's hoping Kyle will be walking out shortly. And if I'm correct, Matt has something to do with the timing. The dude's pussy-whipped over pussy that doesn't even get wet for him. Her sick ass is probably pretending he is Kyle.

I stalk right up to the car. "What are you doing, Beth? You know you're not allowed here," I advise her.

She smirks, then chuckles. I've known chicks like her my entire life—always up to no good. "I'm here to pick up Matt. Is that against the law?" she asks sarcastically.

I step a little closer. "Listen here, you psychotic, stalking skank—I know what you're really up to, but shit isn't going down like that," I warn her. Matt suddenly comes strolling around to the passenger's side of the car.

"Hey, Kins. What's going on?" Matt asks after he gets in and shuts the car door.

I lean over so I can look at him face to face. "Your

friend here has bad intentions. Don't bring her in the vicinity of this place again. I'll have your ass on a stick. Got it?"

His face turns pink. "Yeah, sorry, Kins. I didn't realize this was such an issue," he states.

"She was escorted off the property last year. If Connie saw her here, she would fire you on the spot," I advise him. I then put my attention back to Beth. "I'm going to let you know right now, I see your face around here again, I'm going to *show* you psycho! I'm not afraid to get down and dirty. I'm good at taking out the trash. This is no threat; this is a promise. Understand?"

Beth just huffs and rolls her eyes before screeching off. I hear clapping coming from behind me, and when I turn around, it's Junior. I take a bow. "How long have you been standing here, sunshine?"

"Long enough," he shrugs his shoulders. "You're pretty badass when you're in full motion."

I laugh. "Oh yeah?"

He walks closer to me so we are toe to toe. "That was a big turn-on, Miss Balterson. I want to bend you against this building and fuck the shit out of you from behind," he informs me.

My mouth drops. Yes, he has made me speechless —again! I didn't know he had this in him, and *damn* does that sound so tempting!

"You better clean that dirty mouth before I spank you, Mr. Saunders." Two can play this game. Before either of us can say another word, Elise walks up to us with Jeff.

"What's going on here, guys? Looking pretty intense," Jeff comments with a smug look. I wonder if he knows. Junior doesn't seem like the fuck-and-tell kind, but I've spilled the beans with Max, so I wouldn't put it past him.

"Not much. I just ran Beth off. She came to pick up Matt, and I told her ass to suck it and get lost. Wait until Matt comes back. I still have some words for him," I inform them.

Jeff runs his hand through his hair. "That chick is just crazy! And Matt? What's wrong with that dude? I'm gonna have to have a talk with him."

"Did Max or Kyle see her?" Elise asks.

"No. That's what I was trying to avoid, so I ran out here before either of them came strolling out!" I explain.

Jeff pats me on the back. "I knew you were good for something, Kins."

I give him the evil eye. "You're an ass, Jeff! Elise, you ready?"

"Yup!"

Elise and I order our food and find a table. She looks a bit down, and it's got me a little worried.

"Elise, is everything okay?"

She takes a sip of her iced tea. "I don't know. Jeff has been acting a little weird. He's been distant and pre-occupied. It's just not like him."

My heart melts. "Well, maybe it's just work—or could it be the issues with his father?"

"Actually, he has been speaking with his father by phone on a pretty regular basis now. We're supposed to go visit him and his new wife this summer," she tells me.

The waitress comes over to drop off our food.

"Have you guys been fighting?"

She shakes her head. "No, not at all. Something just feels off," she admits.

I want to go beat his butt! What is wrong with him? He better not screw this up. I'm going to speak with him as soon as we get back to work.

"Elise, I'm sure it's nothing. He adores you. Maybe he's on the rag. Even though they don't bleed, they still get their monthly bitch on."

We both laugh. It's good to see her loosen up a bit.

"How's your mother been?" I ask her.

Her mother was a trainwreck, a pill-popping alcoholic that treated Elise horribly most of her life. Elise kept this secret to herself, not wanting any of us to feel sorry for her. Jeff came into her life at the perfect time. He helped her heal and stand up on her own two feet. I honestly didn't think it was in his DNA. Elise changed him —for the better. They balance each other out perfectly.

"She's actually doing really well. She's now in outpatient rehab but is living in a sort of halfway house. I've been going to AA and NA meetings with her, and we've been doing a lot of family counseling. I just wish she would have done this a lot sooner. She has a lot of guilt from the past, and I'm a little afraid that if she doesn't forgive herself and find a way to move past it all, she might relapse when she's on her own," Elise admits.

That's a huge weight to hold on her shoulders. I don't know how she did it all those years and how she continues to push through.

"I'm glad to hear she's doing well, but I'm more worried about you. How are you handling this all?"

Elise finishes her sub. "Some days are harder than others, especially when we participate in the family counseling, but all I can do is stay hopeful. Jeff is such an amazing support. I wouldn't be able to do any of this without him."

I grab her hand and squeeze. "Elise, you are stronger than you think. Honestly, you're the strongest person I know. Jeff is amazing for being behind you 100 percent, but you also have Max and I. So don't ever feel alone, okay?"

"I know, and thank you for that. You both are such

amazing friends."

We finish up our food. "Okay, enough with the mushy shit! You ready, girl? I swear to God, if I see Beth's car anywhere in the parking lot, I will lose my shit!"

Elise giggles. "If she's smart, she won't be there."

As soon as we get back, I drop my things in my office and storm over to Jeff's cubicle. I want to know what the hell his deal is, and if he realizes Elise is getting upset. I walk up behind him with a powerful urge to smack him upside the head, but I'll keep my hands to myself—for now.

"Jeff."

He turns his seat around. "What's up, Kins?"

I squeeze into his cubicle and lean my butt against his desk so I can look at him eye to eye. He's not getting out of this questioning. I momentarily look around to see who may be able to overhear, but it seems to be pretty cleared out for lunch.

"What's going on with you?"

He looks baffled. "What do you mean?"

"I just came from having lunch with Elise, and she's a little upset. She seems to think something's going on with you, like you're acting different," I break it down to him.

His brows furrow with concern. "Shit! Are you serious?"

"Yes! What the fuck is going on, Jeff? I swear to God, if you're cheating on her, I'm going to castrate you myself!" I threaten.

He shakes his head. "You're freaking insane. I would *never* cheat on her! She's my soulmate, my everything. But listen, there is something going on, but it's not what you think."

"*Okay*—" He needs to spill it already.

"And you have to promise to keep your mouth shut!"

I roll my eyes. "I promise; now what is it?" I demand.

"I bought her an engagement ring, and I'm going to ask her to marry me." My mouth drops. Talk about dropping a bomb. I was so not expecting this!

"Oh my God, Jeff! Are you serious? When are you planning to ask her?"

He exhales. "That's been the problem. I am stressed out trying to find the right moment and the right setting. I choke up every time I want to ask her," he admits, ashamed.

Now I feel guilty for thinking otherwise. "Do you have the ring on you?"

"Yes, I carry it everywhere hoping there might be a special enough moment to drop down on my knee."

I hold out my hand. "Well, let me see it!"

He reaches into his jacket pocket and pulls out the tiny black box. I open it and gasp, putting my hand over my mouth. It's magnificent. "Wow, Jeff, this is beautiful! She is going to absolutely love it. It is so her!" It's one huge, pear-shaped diamond with tiny diamonds along the whole band. It's simple but beautifully stunning.

"Thanks. Junior helped me pick it out," he states. My head snaps up when hearing his name.

"Junior helped?" He nods. A tiny flutter tickles my stomach. "Jeff, listen, Elise doesn't like over-the-top things. Just do it at home when you two are alone. Then you guys can have some crazy engagement sex right after!" I joke, but I really am serious.

"You think?"

"Yes."

He ponders this for a moment. "Maybe you're right; less is better. Okay, tonight is the night then! Thanks, Kins. But do me a favor, keep your mouth shut."

I pat him on his head like a dog. He scowls. I laugh. I couldn't help myself. "You're welcome, and no worries—my mouth is sealed."

The rest of the day goes by slow. We finally got out of the meeting a little after two. The floor was gossiping about my run-in with Beth, which pissed me off, because the only other person around to witness it was Matt. I called him into my office and reamed him a new asshole. He swore up and down it wasn't him and blamed it all on Beth. He said she has an inside source that relays information back and forth, but he has no idea who it is. Yeah, right! This chick takes psycho-stalker to a whole new level.

I am so ready to go home and relax. I walk over to Junior's office and Bridgette is in there. This ought to be good.

I knock on the open door before entering. "Hi Bridgette," I say, quickly switching my attention to Junior. "Are you ready to leave yet?"

He looks a little uncomfortable, but he hands me his car keys. "I'll be out in a minute." I take the keys and leave quietly.

It's been ten minutes, and Junior still isn't out here. Now I'm beginning to get pissed. I would have drove my own car if I knew this crap was going to happen. Just as I'm about to get out of the car, I see him walking out of the office. Boy, he's lucky!

He hops in. "Sorry that took so long. She kind of just barged in my office. I wasn't expecting her."

"Is everything okay?" I ask.

He exhales loudly, then pulls out of the parking lot. "She just came to see if I wanted to do dinner tomorrow night."

Even though I know it's not fair to get jealous, I

still can't help it. I look away so he can't see my face. "Oh? So where are you taking her?"

"I'm not. I told her that I just wanted to stay friends and that I didn't want to lead her on. She was a little upset, but I refuse to be my brother," he explains.

Whoa! I did not want him to break it off for me. I don't want to feel obligated to do the same. Even though I didn't like the idea of him talking to Bridgette, it gave me comfort knowing he wouldn't want something serious with me. "Junior, why in the hell would you do that? You only went on one date with her. You should have given it some time."

He looks annoyed. "Listen, I refuse to lead anyone on. We kissed, and there was no spark. I'm not going to start dating her knowing there's no connection there. And then there's the fact that I'm fucking you on the side. That's not how I roll, Kinsey."

Man, he makes me sound like the devil. Here I am thinking it's great I can date and still bang him on the side. "Okay, I get it. I didn't realize how serious this stuff was to you. Can I ask you something?"

"Sure, shoot."

"Are you going to have a problem with me still seeing Jax?"

He thinks this over for a minute. "I'm not a fan of the idea, but let me ask you something—"

"Okay."

We pull into Chinese Kings to grab some takeout. "If I asked you to stop seeing him, would you?"

Yep, I totally fell into that one. "Nope. But you can be assured that I won't sleep with him, and if I'm considering it, you will be the first to know," I answer honestly.

He rolls his eyes. "Awesome. So does that mean while you're in the middle of the act with him you're going to stop and call me about it?" he asks sarcastically.

I look over to Junior like he's crazy and smack him on his arm. "You're such a dick!"

He chuckles. I love that he's finally starting to get playful. He can be so stiff and dull at times, but there seems to be another side to him that I don't even think he knew he had.

We order our food and head home to veg out in front of the TV. This is going to be a first for Junior and I. We've never sat in this living room together.

I put the food on the coffee table and plant some pillows on the floor for us. Junior grabs the plates and silverware. I grab the remote and search the On Demand channel for a good movie.

This all feels so natural. We move as though we've been together for years. I look over to Junior as he dishes out the rice and sesame chicken, and I feel a calming serenity lather over me. I smile to myself and look away before he notices.

"So, what will it be?" I question as I go through the movie list.

He looks up at the list. "I'm okay with a good chick flick. So choose whatever you want."

"Really? Because I'm a girl you think all I like is chick flicks?"

He laughs. "I don't freaking know. That's why I said pick what you want."

I click my tongue and pick an action movie—

Creed. Junior looks over at me, impressed. I shrug my shoulders. "I'm not a chick flick kind of chick." His eyes twinkle as he smirks. Now, I do love me some Lifetime, but he doesn't need to know that.

"I should have guessed that."

After we finish eating, we sit up next to each other on the couch. This is awkward; we're shoulder to shoulder, tense and unsure of where to go from here. I can't take the weirdness any longer, so I lay my head on the armrest and put my feet on his lap. He holds his hands up for a moment until I get situated, then lies them on my legs. Much better.

We stay like this until the movie ends. The credits are rolling, and other than the music in the background, we remain silent. The energy in the air is charged, and my breath is sporadic as I wait for what's next to come. My body is overly sensitive and dying to be touched. My insides are screaming for him to make the first move.

Usually I need the control, but for tonight, I'm willing to give it up. "Touch me," I whisper to him. This lights a fire under his ass.

He sits up and places my legs on either side of him,

then lies down on top of me between them. We stare at each other for a moment before he leans down to kiss me. My stomach is doing somersaults with just the touch of his lips. My body ignites with an internal fire shooting straight down between my legs.

I run my fingers through his hair and down to his neck to bring him closer into me. I can't seem to get close enough. Junior runs his hand up my thigh to my ass and gives it a big squeeze. I squeal, and we both laugh. I reach the hem of his T-shirt and pull it up over his head, then he begins to unzip his pants and pulls off my shorts and underwear in one quick motion.

I am now completely bare to him. He licks his lips, then looks up to me and smiles. I laugh and put my forearm over my eyes. He is just too damn cute.

Before I can even conjure another thought, his tongue grazes over my clit, and I immediately suck in a breath with pleasure. Damn, it feels *so* good! He rotates his tongue in tiny circles while stroking me with his fingers. I release a moan that I can no longer hold back. He dips two fingers deep into my dripping wet pussy, and I scream out.

His tongue becomes more aggressive with each moan I make, as his fingers slip in and out of me in prefect rhythm.

My body begins to overheat as he builds my orgasm to its peak, and with one last flick of his tongue on my clit, I come tumbling down fiercely. He kisses the inside of my thighs as he works his way back up.

"How was that?" he asks with a mischievous grin. He's knows exactly how good that was.

I shrug. "Not too bad."

"Oh yeah? Okay, you're in for it now, Miss Balterson!"

He kicks off his jeans, then holds the tip of his dick at my entrance. He kisses me deeply, allowing me to taste my own juices, and in one swift movement, he pushes inside of me. "Holy fuck!" I scream. My body still has not come down from the first orgasm, so each pump inside of me is heightened by a thousand. Thank God this boy knows exactly what he's doing!

"God, you feel so fucking good," Junior growls out. He grabs my legs and puts them over his shoulders so he can fuck me harder and deeper. This drives me absolutely insane! I can't hold back any longer, and when I whisper this to him, we both come apart, withering in pure ecstasy.

He releases my legs from his shoulders and comes down to lay his head on my chest. We lie here, still connected, until our breathing slows. He leans up and kisses my neck sweetly.

"Let's go get cleaned up," Junior says, withdrawing from me. We both moan.

He takes my hand and leads me into the bathroom in his room. He turns the water on fiery hot; I can see the clouds of steam pouring out of the shower.

He looks to me before he steps in. "Too hot?"

I shake my head and follow suit. The water feels amazing on my skin. My muscles turn into jelly. He positions me in front of him and then grabs the body soap and rubs it all over. This feels like heaven. I can handle standing here while he cleans me. I could get used to this.

Then it hits me—what Jeff has revealed to me today. "So, I spoke with Jeff today," I inform him.

He stops rubbing me for a moment. "Oh yeah?

About what?" He continues lathering me up.

"About him proposing to Elise."

"He told you?" he asks, surprised.

"Well, I sort of scared it out of him," I admit.

Junior laughs. "What do you mean you scared it out of him?"

I turn around and take the body soap from him to return the favor—only I want to wash the front side of him.

"When I went to lunch with Elise, she said he's been acting weird, and she seemed really upset over it. So when I got back to work, I went to his desk to threaten him, and that's when he came clean."

He just shakes his head. "You are out of control, woman!" he teases. "I went with him to pick out the ring. Did he show it to you?"

"Yep! You guys did a really great job picking it out," I tell him.

"That was all him. I was just there for moral support. I just wonder when it's going to happen."

I lather my hands, then rub his chest and stomach before heading down to his semi-hard dick. Once I grab ahold of it and stroke it a couple of times, it goes stiff like a rod and Junior moans.

I smile, content. "Tonight. I told him to just go for it. So let's hope he does."

I don't think he's listening any longer. He's enjoying my handjob a little too much.

"Damn, Kins, that feels so good!" he hums.

I rinse it off, then drop to my knees. He looks down at me with glazed-over eyes. I grab his cock and begin stroking it again. I rub my tongue in circles over the tip, grab his balls with my other hand, then take him in nice and deep. He groans loudly as his dick touches the back of my throat. I'm enjoying the sound of his bliss; it means I must be doing something right.

I continue to drag my tongue along his vein as I release him, then take him in deep over and over until he can no longer contain his build-up. He cries out as I deplete him of every ounce of his pleasure.

He leans his hands against the shower wall to support his shaky legs. I smile with gratification. He grabs me, wraps his arms around me, and kisses the top of my head. "You're amazing," he says.

CHAPTER NINE

Junior

The week is almost over—finally. I am ready to see what the weekend holds for Kinsey and I. Do we spend the weekend together, or do we just exist as we have every weekend before? I feel as though there's been a change between us, but I'm not too sure what to name it. I'm wondering if she's feeling the same, or am I just reading too much into it?

I got some good sleep last night after our shower session, so I decide to head into work a little early to catch up. I haven't been staying late the last couple of days like I normally do, and I can see the toll it's putting on my work.

My father's always stacked my workload high since I would spend so many extra hours and weekends here. I never minded before, but now that I'm enjoying my time away from work, I'm afraid I may fall behind. I guess I might have to speak with my father about this in the months to come.

It's quiet in here. Only a couple dedicated early-risers. I go to the kitchen to grab some coffee. Shoot! That's reminds me—I never told Kinsey I wouldn't be there for coffee this morning. I would have never cared about something like this before, but all my thoughts seem to be consumed by her now. It's like my brain is going haywire on me. Some sex and a couple of nights with Kinsey has got me all sorts of fucked up.

I grab the cream and sugar.

"Good morning," I hear from behind me. I stiffen just a bit, because I already know whose voice it is.

"Good morning, Bridgette. You're here early."

"Yes, I have some major editing to get done, so here I am, getting some extra time in," she says as she's pouring her coffee. "So, how was the rest of your night?"

Man, this feels pretty uncomfortable after I had to let her down last night.

"It was good. How was yours?" This is like pulling teeth.

Dan from the copy center comes strolling in. I nod

and secretly pray he gets right in between this awkward conversation.

"Weirdly enough, I actually got a call from Jonathan, and we met for some drinks. So, you and Kinsey, huh?" she questions.

I furrow my brows. "Me and Kinsey—what?" I ask, wondering where she is going with this.

"Well, I thought she was dating that guy Jax," she states.

Now I understand. "Oh, I didn't mention to you that we're roommates?"

She looks relieved. "No. *Oh*, so that's why you drove together! I thought maybe you were kind of playing the field or something."

I chuckle. Man, if she even knew. "No, that's not really my thing."

She squeezes my arm. "Good. Now you're not as big of an asshole as I thought," she informs me. Geez, thanks.

I sip my coffee. "Glad to hear it," I express, heading out before she can ask me any more questions.

My head's been stuck in my work for a good hour now. Jeff comes waltzing in with a huge smile on his face, and I can only guess what this is about.

"Did you do it, man?" I ask, excited.

He takes a seat and crosses his leg. "Yup, and she said yes!"

I immediately get up and walk around my desk to give him a hug and slap him up. "Wow! Congratulations, man! Seriously, I am so proud of you!"

"Thanks, bro. I was nervous as hell, but after I had that talk with Kinsey yesterday, I said fuck it and went balls to the wall," he discloses.

I sit back down. "Did she like the ring?"

"She freaking loved it! Max and Kinsey are already talking about throwing her a small engagement party."

I snicker. "Yeah, just wait. It doesn't just stop there. You've opened the whole can of worms now. Just make sure you're the yes man. Just go with it. If you don't, you'll have Max and Kinsey to answer to," I joke, but he knows it's really a true statement.

He exhales. "Shit, you're so right on that."

Speaking of the devil, Kinsey walks through my door. Damn, she looks amazing in that black skirt. All I can picture is lifting it up and fucking her over this desk.

"Good morning, boys," she says. She seems perky and chipper this morning. I wonder why?

"Hey, Kins! Elise is glowing, isn't she?" Jeff asks her.

She laughs. "Yes, Jeff, she is. I was so happy when she called me last night, but Max is a little bummed you didn't tell her ahead of time. I'm just giving you the heads up before you cross paths with her."

"Damn, I didn't even think about that," Jeff swears and then gets up to head to Max's office before she finds him. Kinsey walks around and leans against my desk.

"Where did you go this morning?" she asks with an adorable mischievous smile plastered on her face.

"Sorry, I had some work to catch up on. I'll be here late tonight as well. What are your plans after work?" I wonder.

I love staring into those beautiful baby blues. Shit! I am freaking losing it! "I'm not sure. I need to catch up on some laundry, but I might stop over Max's to see Penelope for a while," Kinsey answers.

At least I don't hear Jax's name in the mix. This makes me a happy man.

"Okay, well I shouldn't be too late. Do you want me to pick something up for dinner?"

She rubs her hand against mine. "No, I'll probably eat something over at Max's. I can bring you home a plate if you want, though?"

"Okay, yeah, that sounds good."

I watch her walk away, and I swear she's putting just a little more oomph in that step. I laugh to myself. I've always avoided looking at her, let alone watching her walk. I secretly knew if I gave in to the temptation, that I might be a goner. So I convinced myself she was annoying and irritating as fuck so I wouldn't fall into her trap. But here I am, somehow becoming prisoner to her existence.

The rest of the day drags on. The girls went out to lunch to celebrate, and judging by the way they were acting, I would think they did a couple of shots, too. I look at the time on my phone, and it's now seven-thirty. I didn't realize I have been here this late. I send Kinsey a quick text letting her know I'm on my way home, and she responds that she's just leaving Max's house with my plate of food.

I feel giddy, like a little kid. I've never been excited to go home before. This is all new to me, and being interested in a woman like Kinsey is most definitely new to me. I usually go for the quieter, reserved type; Kinsey is far from that. But I'm beginning to like the back and forth banter; it keeps things alive and interesting. I didn't realize how mundane my life has become; she's giving my dull world a splash of color and pizazz.

Kinsey is in the shower when I get home. I have the urge to jump right in with her, but I'll chill. I don't want to seem too eager. I go change into my sweats and head back out to the kitchen; she has the plate of food waiting for me.

I take it and go into the living room to watch some TV. A couple minutes later, Kinsey shows up in her tank top and tiny shorts. God, this girl really needs to get some other kind of comfy clothes, because when I see these, I want to do nothing but fuck the shit out of her. I've been avoiding this predicament for months for this very reason.

"Hey, sunshine. What are you watching?" Kinsey asks, sitting down next to me with a glass of red wine.

"Not much, watching a little HBO. This chicken is amazing! Who cooked this? Max?"

She laughs. "No, your brother actually did."

Damn him! I never got the cooking gene. I've tried, but I'm just no good at it. "No shocker there. He seems to have it all."

"Junior, can I ask you something?" Oh boy! I can feel it now. I just opened myself up for a line of questioning.

I continue to watch the TV. "Is it about my brother?"

"Yes."

I finish chewing. "Then I'm not really interested."

Kinsey sits up straight, preparing for a confrontation. I don't give two shits though. I'm not discussing my brother with her.

"Junior, just tell me what happened between you two. Let me help you. I know deep down you both want a relationship with each other, but you're both too busy being stubborn—you especially. Can't you just let the past be and move on from it? Start with a clean slate," Kinsey advises. But I don't need her opinion or assistance with this.

I turn and look at her dead-on. "Listen, Kins, you don't know shit. Just leave it alone," I demand.

"Then help me understand," she begs.

I finish my last bite of food and get up to take the plate to the kitchen. She follows.

"Junior, stop being an ass and just look at me!" Kinsey commands.

I place the plate in the sink loudly and then turn to look at her. "You're fighting a losing battle," I tell her.

She walks up to me and grabs my wrists so I can't walk away. "Then this is a fight I'm willing to lose, because at least I can say I tried, unlike you. Is this all over that girl from high school?"

I chuckle at this ridiculousness. "No, and I told you I'm not discussing this! God, will you just respect my wishes?" I ask, raising my voice. "This isn't your business!"

She lets go of me and crosses her arms over her chest. "We're all close friends, and this is affecting us all, not just the two of you! Kyle already said he's willing to sit down with you and talk this out. Why won't you do the same?"

I suck in and exhale a deep breath to calm myself so I don't lose it on her. "Kinsey, just drop it, okay?" I attempt to ask her nicely.

"Err," she growls before walking away. "You are so damn frustrating, Junior! You really make me want to knock you out!" she finishes, stomping toward the living room.

Even though I am aggravated as hell with her, watching her walk away in those tiny shorts just does something to me. I run after her and lift her over my shoulder before she even realizes what's going on. She begins to kick and scream for me to put her down. I smack her on her ass and head down the hall to my room.

I reach my bed and throw her ass down. She sits up

in rare form. "What the fuck, Junior?" she yells. I take my shirt off and then drop my pants. She immediately shuts up. Now I have her attention, because she sure has my cock at full attention.

She squints at me with anger. "You're a bastard, you know that? You just don't play fair!" she states.

I reach down and slide her shorts and underwear off. I spread her legs and kneel down in between them. She watches me intently, her chest heaving up and down, without saying another word.

I run my fingers up and down the middle of her pussy, then up to her clit where I apply the tiniest pressure. She sucks in a breath of air and arches her back. Every part of her is so beautiful. My tongue is dying to taste her again.

I lean down and place tiny kisses along the inside of her leg until I reach her glistening wet lips. I lick from her ass all the way up to her clit. She moans and squirms. I hold her hips in place and repeat; she tastes so good.

I insert my fingers deep inside of her while circling her with my tongue. I want to taste all of her pleasure. "Come for me," I demand.

She grabs hold of the comforter as her moans become louder. I accost her most intimate parts with all I have until she comes apart over my tongue. I kiss her all the way up to her lips. "You taste like heaven," I whisper.

She rolls me over so she is now on top, straddling me. I lift up her shirt and unsnap her bra so all I see is skin. I've never seen anything so beautiful. How did I get so lucky?

Kinsey leans down for a kiss and nips at my bottom lip. I'm so hard, I'm ready to combust. I grab her hips and lift her over my dick. She slowly sinks down on me, and my eyes roll back into my head. I'm in pure heaven.

She feels so warm and slick against my skin. "Are you ready?" she asks me seductively. I nod eagerly. She places her palms on my chest and begins moving over me like a wild lioness. I let her take full control, and I just enjoy the ride—and let me tell you, this is one hell of a ride.

Every muscle in my body is telling me that it's time to release, but I just want to enjoy it a bit longer. I grind my teeth together, close my eyes, and try to think of something unpleasant. But as soon as I open my eyes and see this gorgeous beauty on top of me, everything comes crumbling down.

Why didn't I do this sooner?

Kinsey lays her head on my chest once she's finished. "So Mr. Saunders, are you ready to talk?" she asks.

Damn it! Does she really have to do this right now? I roll her over and get up to clean myself. I grab her a towel from my bathroom, then I throw my boxer briefs back on.

"Sure, we can talk about anything *but* Kyle."

She rolls her eyes. I crawl back into bed with her and bring her into me. She stiffens momentarily as her back touches my chest and I nuzzle into her neck.

"Just relax, Kins. Doing this doesn't mean we're in a relationship. We're just two people enjoying a moment together after great sex," I explain to her so she doesn't flee.

She finally relaxes. "Okay, tell me about your

relationship with your parents then."

I inhale the scent of her hair. "We've always had a good relationship. My father wasn't around much when I was growing up; he worked himself to the bone. But my mother was there for every monumental moment, and she made sure Dad was there for the most important stuff.

"I was the oldest, so my father depended on me to look out for Kyle. I hated that, because every time he would get in trouble, it was somehow a reflection on me, because I didn't prevent it," I tell her.

"That must have been hard. Did he get in trouble a lot?"

I entwine my fingers with hers. "Did he ever! He and Jeff were bad together. They skipped school, got wasted at parties, and let's not talk about the line of girls just waiting to have their hearts broken. It was sickening. Any extra time my dad had at home was spent running around after Kyle and dealing with his foolishness.

"I missed out on one-on-one time growing up, but we made up for lost time when we started working together," I finish.

"He called me in his office the other day regarding my Sampson client, but before I left, he asked me how everything was going here at the apartment and if we needed anything. I got the impression he was digging around for something more," she discloses.

I chuckle. "Yes, I bet he was. My mother's been on my back about dating. I had to tell her to chill out; I'm sick of hearing it. So, my guess is she has recruited my dad to get on the dating train as well. My mom's always asking about you. She adores you."

She turns her head to look at me. "Really? She's great. I miss my parents like crazy. I'm actually leaving next weekend to go visit them."

My breath catches. I'm a little caught off guard. "For how long?" I ask.

She turns back around. "A week."

A freaking week? Damn, this sucks. But it also means a Jax-free week for Kinsey, and I'm good with that. "That's cool. I bet your parents are excited to see you."

"Yes, my mom is already planning girl time. Oh shit!" she swears, smacking her forehead.

I laugh. "What?"

"I told Jax I was free next weekend, totally forgetting I was leaving. He said he wanted me for his date to some work event he has to attend," she informs me. Yeah, this is not what I wanted to hear while she's lying in my arms, in my bed, after we just got done having sex.

"Oh yeah?" is all I seem to be able to get out.

"Damn! I'm sorry, boo. This was totally the wrong place and time to mention that. I wasn't thinking," she apologizes. I'm sure I won't be getting many of those from her, so I'm going to savor that apology.

"Shh," I say to quiet her, kissing her neck. I don't want to talk anymore. I just want to be. I lean behind me and shut off the light. "Just stay with me tonight," I whisper to her.

CHAPTER TEN

Kinsey

I wake up, crushed, with legs and heavy arms wrapped around me. I'm trapped, and I don't like this. I feel claustrophobic. It's pitch dark except for the low light coming from the bathroom. I carefully roll out of Junior's grip so I don't wake him and tiptoe out of his room to mine. Once I reach my room, I shut the door quietly and take a deep breath. I've been holding my breath this whole time. I feel a little guilty for leaving his room, but I said I would stay the night with him, and it's now five in the morning.

I jump into my bed and completely bury myself in my covers. I am royally fucked up. I don't know how to fully let someone in any longer. Being wrapped in Junior's arms throws me off-kilter, and I don't like feeling helpless or vulnerable. Once feelings from the past creep up, I have no choice but to lock and bolt myself tightly closed.

I finally fall back asleep, only to be woken up two hours later by the alarm clock. My eyes are dry and burning. I feel as though my brain hasn't even shut down since I came back into my room. Screw coffee at home. This calls for some Starbucks crack coffee. It's going to be the only thing to put a dent in my exhaustion. All this sex is wearing me out. Geez, I never thought I would ever say those words.

I drag myself into the shower, which helps me wake up some. By the time I get dressed and complete my morning routine, it's almost eight. I walk into Junior's room to make sure he's not still sleeping; I haven't heard a peep from him. But his room is empty, and he's nowhere to be found.

I head into work after grabbing my coffee and go straight to my office. Today is going to be a rough one. Max called in because Penelope is sick, which means I have to pick up her work for the day as well.

I still haven't seen Junior since last night, and to be honest, I feel sort of like an ass for bolting on him. But this is what I do; I panic and then I run. Of course, this situation is just a bit different considering I'm living with the man I want to run from. Smart move, Kins.

After a couple of hours locked in my office, I decide to visit Junior at his office. He looks like he's in major concentration mode. I knock on the outer part of his door and invite myself in. "How's it going, sunshine? You look pretty busy there—"

He looks up at me with a cold and distant look. Ouch. Okay, okay, he's definitely pissed at me. "I am. What do you want, Kinsey?" he questions.

Shit! "You're mad at me, aren't you?" I ask, cringing. Let's just get it right out in the open; no sugar-coating it.

"That's understating it. I woke up, and you were gone," he says angrily. "What's your deal? What the hell are you afraid of?"

This is the wrong place to get into all of this, but maybe it's time I tell him about my past. "You're right. I'm terrified. Waking up next to you made me panic. I completely freaked out. You didn't deserve that, but the truth is, Junior, we're still getting to know each other. I'm not looking to fall in love. I like fucking you, but I just can't deal with the mushy, romantic shit. If that's what you need, then I'm not the woman you should be with," I tell him honestly before getting up to leave.

Screw telling him about my past. What's the point in him knowing anyway? It's just more ammo to use against me in the long run. "I'll be going to Max and Kyle's for dinner tonight, will you be there?"

He turns back to his work, completely shutting me out. "No, I have to work late again tonight."

I see the old Junior has now returned, and it's my fault. I caused it. I turn to head back to my office. Whatever we had has now been tainted. Damn, me and my mouth. I didn't even mean for it to come out like that! I'm such an asshole!

The workday has finally ended, and I head over to Max's. I have to catch her up on what she missed today. I stopped at the liquor store to grab a bottle of wine. After dealing with a sick little girl, I know she could use a glass.

It smells delicious when I step into her house. I head into the kitchen. "It smells amazing! Did you cook this?" I ask Max.

She has sauce and meatballs simmering and pasta

cooking on the stove. "Yuppers! This is actually Kyle's recipe. I decided to surprise him with it," she answers while cutting some fresh bread.

I look around. "Where is Kyle?"

"He's upstairs, changing."

I hold up the bottle of wine and take a seat at her dining room table.

She takes the bottle from me and hugs it with her life. "You are a lifesaver! I *so* needed this."

"How's Penelope feeling?"

Max grabs a wine opener. "Her fever has gone down some, but it's because of the Motrin. She finally let me put her down for a nap; she was my cuddle buddy all day."

I just love how Max has become so domesticated. I wish I could see myself this way, but I just can't get past my fear and anxiety caused by my past. I know all men aren't like Tommy, but knowing this still doesn't make it any easier. What happens when Junior gets sick of me? If I fall for him and he tosses me aside, how will I be able to face him on the daily?

"Ok, so have you thought any on making a date for the wedding?" I bug her. She's been engaged for months now, and they still haven't set a date.

She huffs. "No, we've just been so busy! But, Kyle did have an idea—"

I start jumping up and down in my seat. "Oh my God! What is it? Spill it, now!"

She cracks up. "He mentioned maybe heading out to Vegas for a weekend and doing it there."

My brows furrow as I take this all in. "Is that something you want to do? What about Kyle's parents? What about your brothers?" I question.

She pours our glasses of wine. "I don't know yet. It was just an idea, but of course they all would be invited to come."

I hear footsteps from behind me. "Hey, Kins," Kyle greets. "Did Junior come with you?"

I'm a little surprised he asked. "Nope. Junior is acting pissy with me today."

He chuckles. "When is he not?" he jokes. "What did you do this time?"

"I left his bed before he woke up," I admit. Kyle almost spits out the water he just sipped.

"What? You have got to be joking with me!" he then looks to Maxine. "Max, did you know about this?"

Her face turns pink. "Um, kind of. I didn't know it was an everyday thing though," she responds. "I'm sorry, babe; sometimes a girl has to keep a girl's secret."

Kyle keeps trying to say something, but nothing comes out. "Kyle, your brother and I are just friends who have occasional sex sometimes—well more than sometimes—but that's beside the point," I tell him. "I told him this morning that I'm not looking for love, and I'm not into the cuddling crap."

He looks at me like I have lost my mind. "You really said that to him?"

"Yes, I really said that. I'm always honest, even if it hurts. Someday he will thank me," I answer.

"Aww, Kins! You gotta stop pushing everyone away. Junior doesn't just invite people into his life so easily. If he's let you in, it's because he's really into you," Max informs me.

Kyle jumps back in. "Max is right, you know. When it comes to women, he is extremely picky. I'm honestly shocked he's chosen you." Both Max's and my mouth drops. "Wait, wait, I mean he has made it abundantly clear how much you drive him crazy, and Junior doesn't do crazy," he explains.

Okay, I can accept that explanation. "Actually, Junior has let loose some. He's kind of fun to hang with. I didn't think he had it in him, but I really like being around him now. I admit, I can be a total ass—"

"You can say that again!" Kyle says.

I shake my head and scowl at Kyle. "Maybe I shouldn't have been so abrupt with him, but to tell you the truth, he scares me. I feel things that I haven't felt in a long time, and I don't like it. So I guess Max is right; I push men away. I feel like if I get too close than that gives them power: power to hurt me, power to destroy my world."

Max walks over to give me a hug. She knows every dirty detail possible of my life, and thank God she doesn't pillow talk like most girlfriends do. I can trust her completely. She is truly my soul sister.

"You know what, Kins? Just talk to him. Tell him what you've just told me. Even though my brother and I don't get along, I know him, and I know he will understand why you are the way you are," Kyle counsels me. Who would have ever thought?

"Maybe you're right, but to be honest, he shut me down when it came to you. He straight-up refused to discuss anything that had to do with you. I mean, we actually got into a confrontation over it. I honestly think he's been mad at you for so long that he doesn't even remember the initial cause," I tell him.

Kyle mulls this over for a moment before replying. "I think you're right, Kins. Maybe I just need to step up and confront him on this."

"What about Monday night? You guys can come over for some pizza and beers, and Max and I can disappear for a while so you can speak with him. This way he won't suspect a thing," I plot.

"Oooh, yes! That's a good idea. But this means you need to make nice with Junior over the weekend so he won't stay late at work," Max advises, taking a sip of her wine.

I huff loudly. Oh, yes. I forgot about that small pain-in-the-ass detail. He's so hard to get through to when he shuts down. I'm still learning all his buttons and what makes him tick. He is one complicated guy to figure out. This is going to take some skilled planning on my end.

"I think I can work on that. If it's an epic fail, I will let you two know," I inform them.

Kyle starts following his nose to the saucepot. He lifts the cover, grabs a spoon, and tests the sauce Max just slaved over. "Mmm, damn baby! That is some good sauce!" Kyle tells her before kissing her neck and wrapping his arms around her. She becomes putty in his hands. I absolutely love the way he loves her. If only I could allow myself to let people in. Old and alone is how I picture myself in the future.

"I can't wait to taste it!" I add.

The rest of the night goes by fast. I swear I had to roll myself out of their house to get into my car. I ate so much that I am ready to combust.

It's now eight o'clock, and when I enter the

apartment, it's quiet; the only light on is the one over the kitchen sink. I saw Junior's car parked in the garage, so he must have gone to bed already. There goes my plan of defrosting his cold, frozen self.

Maybe I can still make this happen. I'm sure if I walked into his room, crawled under his covers to give him the best head in the world, he may forgive me for my reckless mouth earlier. But this still doesn't sound good enough. I mean, what would possibly happen if I was to let him in about my past? Yes, he could hurt me or maybe find me pathetic or use it against me. But maybe, just maybe, he may understand as a friend would, and he might be able to accept my faults.

Unfortunately, I have many of them. I either end up scaring people away or pushing them away. Either way, they never stick around long enough to know the true me behind this loud, big mouth.

I digest for a bit, then I get changed into my tank and shorts that Junior loves so much and head over to his room. I crack the door open and can hear the low snore coming from him. The bathroom light is on a dull setting, just enough for me to see his outline.

I've decided to take a big leap. I figure if he realizes I am trying to open up just a tad, then maybe he may do the same for me. I crawl under the covers next to him to fall asleep. I don't rustle him or wake him, because I'm hoping when he opens his eyes, he will accept my unsaid apology.

I lie here awhile, just listening to Junior sleep peacefully, and eventually his rhythmic breathing lulls me to sleep.

"Kins! Wake up!" a voice says in the distance. Then comes a nudge. "Kins, what are you doing in my bed?" the voice asks. Then comes a harder nudge. My eyes flutter open, only to see Junior leaning over me, confused. I thought I was dreaming. Oh yes, the plan.

I reach for his face to bring his lips down to mine, but he doesn't follow. He removes my hands from him so he can back up just a tad. My heart sinks just a bit from the rejection.

This time I run my finger down the side of his cheek while gazing into his curious eyes.

"What are you doing?" he asks softly.

"I wanted to say sorry for earlier, but I didn't know how. You were already sleeping when I got home, so I wanted to be here this time when you woke up. I'm not very good at apologizing, so I thought I'd show you instead of telling you," I explain.

He doesn't say another word. He slowly leans down and touches his lips to mine. Every strand of hair on my body is now standing straight up. The energy surrounding us intensifies by ten. Junior coaxes my mouth open with his tongue, and I happily comply. Our tongues graze and play, then rescind.

He begins kissing and nipping at my neck. Each tug of my skin jolts straight down between my thighs. He grabs my wrists and brings them above my head. I haven't seen this feisty, playful side yet, but I'm liking it. He holds both wrists with one hand tightly in place as his other hand slides down my side, over my hip. He then dips his fingers under my panties, plunging deep into me. I cry out, unable to help myself. He knows just the right spot to hit.

I grind myself over his fingers. "Does that feel good?" he whispers. I nod.

As soon as he rubs over my clit, I arch my back and let out a whimpering moan. The things this man can do with his fingers—but I can't let him have all the fun. I roll him over, with his fingers still inside of me, so I am now on top.

We gaze at each other for a moment. He removes his fingers from me, then he puts them in his mouth to suck on them. I draw in a breath. That was a pretty bold but extremely hot move. I center myself over his stiff cock, then sink myself down right on it, filling myself to the hilt.

Junior groans loudly as his eyes roll back into his head. I smile with satisfaction. I lock my hands with his and begin my womanly assault on him. Every movement brings us closer to ecstasy; building and climbing to the peak until we both tip over the edge.

My body shakes as my orgasm subsides. He's taken everything from me, and my muscles are now like Jell-O. I lay my head on his chest as he runs his fingers up and down my spine.

"That was the best apology you could ever give me. Can you make sure to always apologize like that?" Junior teases.

I laugh. It does funny things to me since we're still connected. He's just too much. Who would have ever thought I would be laughing at anything he has to say? "So, does this mean we're going to be fighting a lot more?" I tease back.

"Only if you come into my office again and read me my rights. You were pretty harsh," he tells me. I try to move off of him, but he holds me in place. "Kins, I know there's something you're not telling me, something that's molded you into the way you are today, and I just want you to know I would never judge you. We all have stories and things that we've been through; it only makes us human, Kins. So, when your ready to share, I will be ready to listen. Your secrets are safe with me."

"So are we really doing this after-sex mushiness?" I ask.

He smacks his arm over his eyes. "God, Kins, I

swear you are just impossible! I really think you should have been born as a man. I mean, thank God you weren't, but what the hell? It's like you were born without an emotional bone in your body!"

I laugh. He groans, and again it does funny things to my now tingling area that is still connected with his. I disconnect from him and walk toward the bathroom to clean myself up.

"Being emotional is just not really my thing, boo," I yell from the bathroom. I throw him a towel so he can clean up and then slide back into his bed.

He rolls to his side so he can talk to me face-to-face. "Then tell me what your 'thing' is."

I look him straight in the eyes. "Fucking," I say bluntly.

He runs his fingers down my cheek. "What am I going to do with you?"

I scooch over so I can lay my head on his chest. This isn't so bad. He kisses the top of my head and reaches to turn off the lamp light. I close my eyes and take a deep breath, allowing his heartbeat to take me away.

CHAPTER ELEVEN

Junior

I crack my eyes open, expecting the other half of my bed to be empty and cold, but it's not. Kinsey is still lying next to me, wrapped in my arms. I thought I would never see this day. She looks beautifully peaceful, and I'd like to think I had a part in this.

I carefully slide out from under her so I don't wake her and head toward the shower. I turn to look at her one last time, to burn this picture in my memory, because I have no idea if this will ever happen again. Her caramel brown hair fans over my navy blue pillow, making her look angelic and innocent, but this thought only lasts so long, because memories of her tyrant ways from early this morning shine brightly in my head.

After I shower, I leave her sleeping in my bed. It's Saturday, and I'm forcing myself into work for a couple of hours to get some overdue work done.

The office is quiet, and I think the only other person in here is my mother. I walk over to her office. "Hey, Ma. Don't you ever sleep in on the weekends?"

I take a seat in front of her desk.

"Nope. There's just too much to do. Anyways, your father got up to play some golf. He caused so much ruckus that there's was no way I was getting back to sleep," she tells me. She looks at me more closely. "You look like you didn't get much sleep," she comments. "Is everything okay?"

"Yeah, everything's great. I've just been a little preoccupied," I tell her honestly.

She smiles that all-knowing mom smile. No matter how much I want to keep from her, she always knows. It's a mother's intuition.

"Well, if you're not going to be sleeping too much at night, make sure you fit in a nap," she responds. "Hey, listen, have you spoken with your brother?"

Come on! She already knows the answer to this question. "I'm just wondering if you've heard anything about the wedding. They still haven't set a date yet."

"Mom, just give them time. A long engagement is not a horrible thing. They just had the baby, and they both work like crazy. Oh, did you hear that Jeff proposed to Elise?" I ask.

She sits up nice and straight with excitement. "Yes! I did! I am so happy for Jeffery, and that Elise is such a doll!"

"Well, now we have two weddings to be looking forward to," I tell her before getting up to head out. "Okay, I got a lot of work to do. I'll talk to you later. Maybe you and Dad can come over for dinner sometime this week. Kinsey is a great cook."

"Yes, let us know. We would absolutely love to!" she says ecstatically.

I head to the kitchen to grab some coffee, then I lock myself in my office for the rest of the day. I check my phone periodically to see if Kinsey texts—but nothing.

It's now quarter to four. My neck is stiff and my back aches from sitting so long. I know Kinsey has a date tonight with Jax; I just don't know what time. Damn! I should have asked. Maybe if I leave now I can see her before she leaves. Of course, I'm not so sure I should see her before her date. I already know it's going to crush me.

I rush home and storm through the door, only to see Jax sitting down on the barstool in my apartment. My gut sinks. I make sure to suck back any emotions when he comes up to me to shake my hand.

"Hey, Junior. It's nice to see you, man."

I shake his hand very firmly. "Yeah, same," I hate being cordial when I want to rip someone's face off. "You waiting on Kins?"

"Yup, she said she just had to finish up quickly," he replies, sitting back down on the stool—on *my* stool.

"I'll go see if she's ready for you." I head toward her room before he can say another word.

I knock on her door quickly, then I open it before she can respond. I don't care if she's ready or if she's even dressed. I shut the door behind me, and she looks at me like I'm crazy.

"Um, what are you doing, Junior?" she questions, confused.

I don't say a word. I walk over to her, spin her in her makeup chair, and kiss her with every ounce of passion I can muster up. She tries to push me away at first, but I push back harder and she gives in. I want to have the taste of my lips on hers, the smell of my body on hers, and thoughts of me on her mind when she leaves with *him*.

"Junior—" Kinsey says in between kisses.

I finally let go of her to give her space.

"Junior, you can't do this! Jax is right outside!" she screeches quietly.

She looks beautiful. I'm just glad she has on jeans and not a dress. "You know this is killing me, right?" I admit.

She pokes her bottom lip out, feeling bad for me. "You weren't supposed to be here. I thought you would still be at work."

"I wanted to come see you before you left with him. When will you be back?" I know I shouldn't ask, but it just rolled off my tongue.

She stands up and points to the door. "Out! Or Jax is going to wonder what we're doing in here alone for so long. I'd rather not tell my date that I'm in here making out with my roommate."

I chuckle. "Okay, fine. I just had to let you know what you're leaving behind," I tease her.

"Don't worry, I'll be back later for that," she tells me. This makes me smirk before I walk out.

I lock eyes with Jax. "She's almost ready," I tell him as I go into the kitchen to grab a glass of wine. I hold up the bottle. "Would you like a drink?"

"No, I'm good. Thanks."

I just shrug. He looks at me as though he wants to ask me something but isn't sure if he should.

"So, how long have you and Kinsey known each other for?" he finally asks.

I lean my butt against the counter to face him. "About two years now. Her best friend is basically married to my little brother," I tell him.

"Ah, gottcha. Well, lucky you; you get to bunk with a hot chick," he comments.

I never told Kinsey this, but my friend Jonas, who bounces at The Tavern, asked me if I knew Jax well. He told me Jax comes in a lot to see the bartender, Jessica, and they've left a couple of times together. I should have said something to Kinsey, but if I did, she may have thought I was just acting jealous and overreacting.

"So, are you dating Jessica as well?" I ask.

Jax leans his head to the side. "Jessica?"

"Yes, the bartender from The Tavern. My friend is the bouncer there and says you're there a lot," I inform him.

I can see the wheels turning in his head. "Yeah, I go in there with people from work, and Jessica usually just happens to be working on those days," he replies. I can feel the tension beginning to build between us.

I'm done with the tiptoeing around this. "Let's cut the bullshit," I tell Jax directly.

"Excuse me?" he says.

I finish my sip of my wine. "I know your type. *Believe* me, I *know* your type. You're not fooling me. Come on man, you've left with Jessica on numerous occasions. I don't know what you want from Kinsey, but I'm not going to let you hurt her," I advise him. Before I can say another word, Kinsey comes out.

"Hey, I'm ready!" she says to Jax with a huge smile. Her face drops as soon as she senses the tension. "What did I miss?"

Jax stands up quickly and slaps a fake smile on his face. "Nothing. We need to get going, or we're going to be late for the movie."

She looks back to me with her brows furrowed. I just shake my head to reassure her. There's no way I'm going to give Jax the satisfaction of ruining Kinsey's night. Once she's done with him, she'll be back home where she belongs, with me.

The door shuts behind them, and I am left alone with my silence. This sucks. I look around, not knowing what to even do with myself. I drag myself over to the couch and turn on the TV. I want to be here waiting when she comes back.

CHAPTER THIRTEEN

Kinsey

Jax seems a little uptight. Usually he's talkative and spunky, but tonight—nothing. "Is everything okay?" I ask.

He doesn't even open the door to his SUV for me this time. "Yeah, I'm good, but your roommate seems to be a bit territorial."

I turn to him. "What do you mean?"

He shakes his head. "It was nothing. Just guy talk."

I'm not buying it. "It was clearly something, or you would have never brought it up."

He reaches over and places his hand on my hand. "He just warned me to treat you good. I think he has a serious thing for you," he tells me. Geez, if he only knew.

I look away from him, out the front window. The streets are alive tonight. Usually this would excite me, because I love being out and about where chaos is happening. But this truck is full of tension. "He's just protective, because of our friends. We all work closely together, too. He's really a great guy."

"Should I be concerned about him?" he questions.

Yes, yes you should be. "No, you have nothing to worry about. We're just roommates," I lie. I think my nose just grew twelve inches.

He squeezes my hand. "Okay, good."

"I never asked you: what are we going to see?"

"I thought we would go see *The Walls of the Heart.* I've heard it's really good," he tells me. It sounds like garbage. This almost comes ripping out of my mouth, but I control myself.

"So, it's a chick flick, right?"

He chuckles. This irritates me. "Yeah, I guess it is."

"So, because I'm a chick, I automatically love romantic, sob-filled movies?" I question, maybe being a little too harsh, but I don't really care. "Jax, you're a lawyer for God's sake! You're never supposed to assume. Facts are what you live by, so let me give you a hint—this 'chick' over here is not like all the others. The mushy love shit just makes me want to gag, honestly. So, we can go see it if you're okay with me upchucking all over your shoes," I finish. Maybe I'm being a little too dramatic, but damn, first Junior and now him? And having a million sisters is no excuse either. I don't have "fragile" stamped all over my goddang head, do I?

He laughs. "Okay, okay, I'm sorry. I should have asked what you wanted to see. I'm sure there's other movies playing. We can choose something else when we get there," he says, shaking his head.

I crack a half-smile. I don't know if it's me, Jax, or the tension running through the air that's making me a little nutty, but I allow it to melt off so I can give him a reassuring smile.

"Well, thank you. I appreciate that, and I didn't mean to jump down your throat," I tell him without having to say sorry. I hate apologizing.

We pull up to the movie theater and park. There's kind of a weird silence happening between us. It's not something I'm really used to. Usually my mouth is pretty good at filling the void. We get up to the ticket counter and take a moment to look at the movies.

We have about ten minutes before *Landslide* plays. It's supposed to be an action-filled movie. I need something to pump me up, because so far this date is a little on the dull side. We grab our drinks and popcorn, and find a seat in the back of the theatre. "So, is this a little better, Miss Kinsey?" Jax asks.

I shove a handful of popcorn in my mouth and nod my head; I'm just really not in the mood to talk. Maybe this movie will inspire some sort of conversation flow once it's finished. The lights dim down, the trailers start, and Jax's arm now slides behind me. He must know this move very well.

There's a young couple below us that become pretty hands-on with each other, which quickly evolves into a full-blown makeout session. When I last checked the screen, there were bombs and AK-47s going off, not Mr. Boombostic sex music playing. These kids have no qualms about their surroundings.

The movie ends, and it was actually really good. "You ready?" Jax offers me a hand out of my seat.

"Yup. My butt was getting numb!" He laughs while

holding my hand down the dark stairs. "So, where to now?"
I ask.

We cram out the double doors like sardines. "I
thought we would go back to my place, and I can cook us
some dinner—"

"Just so we're clear—this is dinner, not an attempt
to get me in bed, right?" I ask bluntly. I'm not into the
whole seducing thing tonight. I know the idea is bound to
come up at some point, but tonight I just want to relax.
Besides, I have a hot, steamy man waiting for me at home.
Shit! I sound so freaking skanky. Am I a skank? Damn, if I
were to explain this situation to a complete stranger, they
would definitely be calling me a skank in their heads.

Jax looks at me a little cockeyed. "*Me*, try to have
sex with *you?*" he says sarcastically. Okay, I may have
deserved that. "Kinsey, you need to relax a little. It's just
some dinner and conversation—if you're okay with that, of
course."

I loosen up a bit. This time he opens the car door
for me, and we head off to his place. We pull into a parking
garage downtown—it's actually not too far from my place

—and we go through the front doors where the bellman waits to take us up the elevator. I didn't know places still did this anymore. Weird.

His loft is pretty grand. It's very contemporary and has an extremely sterilized feeling to it, overly clean and almost museum-like. I'm guessing he doesn't have time to do this all himself.

"Wow, Jax. This place is *really* nice. How long have you lived here for?" I ask as I give myself a tour around the place.

He heads into the kitchen. "About two years now," he yells after I walk down the hallway. He has two bedrooms and an office. I peek in the rooms but don't walk in.

I head back to the kitchen. "This place is really massive for just you. Did you plan on having a roommate?"

He holds up a bottle of wine in one hand and a bottle of Grey Goose in the other. I point to the wine. He grabs the wine opener and begins to uncork it. "Actually, I was going to have a roommate, but it didn't work out. I could have chosen to move, but I like it here. The neighbors are quiet and the security is great, but the best part is that it's not far from my office."

"What happened with the roommate situation?" I ask. He hands me my wine.

He begins prepping the food. "It was a buddy I went to law school with. His girlfriend and him split up after five years together. He was attempting to move on, and I was looking for a place, so it just fit. Right before we were going to move in, they reconciled and he went back home with her. I was just glad to see them back together."

He begins to wash the asparagus. "Well, good for them. Do you need any help?"

He shakes his head. "No. I told you I was cooking for you. So you just look pretty and keep sipping on that wine," he directs.

He looks down to his phone after it's gone off for the third time in the last twenty minutes. It's clear someone is really trying to get ahold of him. He shoots a text back and puts the phone back down. I'm curious, but it's not really my business yet to ask him who it is.

"You don't have to tell me twice!" I giggle. "So you

told me you were in a serious relationship with Jessica's sister; have you been in any others since?" I question.

He begins slicing the steak in thin strips. "Nope. I started working at the firm, and I got preoccupied with court cases. I've been dating, but nothing serious. How about you?"

I take a sip of courage. "I haven't really had a serious relationship since high school. I guess, like you, work's been my number one priority. I actually may start writing in my free time," I announce.

He looks up at me with a smile. "Oh yeah? That's great. What exactly do you want to write?"

He places the strips in the frying pan to give them a quick sear. "I like fiction; maybe romance of some type. I guess I really won't know until I sit down to write. I still really don't know if I'm going to do this or not. It's a hard world for authors out there. I have to send out thousands of rejection emails a month to authors, so I should know. It crushes me to know each one of those letters could potentially cause a writer to give up on their dreams."

"Wow, I never thought of it like that. That's a hard

burden to carry around with you."

"Yes, that's very true, but the good outweighs the bad. We discover so many amazing new writers every day. Some of them are just so gifted with words. That's why I love what I do. So I don't think I'll ever fully give up on working side by side with these agents, but who knows what the future holds for me," I finish. I'm shocked. I really haven't shared this with too many people. Why Jax? I have no idea.

He throws the asparagus in the pan with the steak and starts preparing the salad. I've almost downed half of my wine. My ass needs to slow it down before I get *too* loosened up.

"It sounds like whatever decision; it'll be a great one. You're already doing something you love, so anything else will just add to it. I never seem to deal with girls who have it all together. This is a first for me, and I have to say, it's a real turn-on. Of course, that sassy mouth of yours just adds to it all," he says, giving me a wink.

Boy, this date started out pretty rocky, but it's now heading in the right direction. I find myself enjoying his flirtatious wink. "Well thank you, Mr. Jax. Hey, I don't think you've ever told me your last name—"

He squints at me. "If I tell you, I may have to kill you," he jokes.

"Hmm, I think that can be arranged: death by book," I wink back.

"It's James," he says with a smile.

After another ten minutes or so, the food is ready. He brings our plates over to his table. I grab the drinks and silverware. He lights the two candles in between us and walks over to dim the lights. Wow, this is definitely a top-notch, romantic date. I feel intensely guilty, because Junior keeps popping up in the back of my mind. Is it weird that part of me feels as though I'm cheating on him? Or would I technically be cheating on Jax?

He waits for me to take my first bite, and man, oh man, is it delicious!

"Wow, Jax, this is really amazing! And the asparagus still has a crunch to it! I hate when it's all soggy."

He starts to dig into his. "Same here. I think that's a pet peeve of mine. I'm glad you like it."

His phone goes off again, but he doesn't bother to get up to look. Now I'm getting extremely curious. "Is everything okay?" I ask.

His brows furrow, confused. "Yeah, why?"

"Well, your phone seems to be going off like crazy tonight. If you need to call them back, I won't take any offense to it," I tell him.

He doesn't even take the time to consider my offer. "No, it's fine. It's nothing important."

He doesn't divulge any more information than that, which pretty much tells me it's none of my business. I can accept that. We're not serious, so there's no need for him to feel pressured to tell me anything.

Of course, once this happens, my phone goes off. I get up to grab my purse. The text is from Junior, asking how everything's going. I shoot him a quick text back that everything is fine, and I'll be back home later. Damn, this whole thing is just an odd mess.

Jax doesn't ask me about the text, and we go back to where we left off. He pours me my second glass of wine before he clears off the table. I offer to help, but he's not having it.

"I'll be right back," he says, heading to the restroom.

"Okay."

I look around and smile. I'm actually enjoying myself, and I'm extremely content at the moment. I honestly don't want to leave yet. And again, here comes the wave of guilt cresting over me. I really have nothing to feel guilty about when it comes to Junior. I have been 100 percent honest with him, and he's the one who is choosing to wait. When it comes to Jax, we haven't even come close to committing to each other exclusively, so my conscience is clear there.

I see some crumbs on the table, so I head to the kitchen to grab a sponge. His phone's sitting on the counter next to the sink. It goes off, but I ignore it. Then it goes off again, and I'm curious. I lean over it and see a text from Jessica come across the screen.

It says, "You can't ignore me after the other night together."

Then another text come through, "Are you with

her? I'm on my way over."

I'm frozen. We had this great night together, he told me he wasn't seeing her, and the worst part is that he brought me into the place where she works and strutted me around in front of her. How cruel.

I hear him walking down the hallway, and I quickly walk over to my purse on the counter to grab my phone. Jessica is on her way, and he has no clue. This isn't my battle to fight, and I'll be damned if I'm going to stay to watch it.

I text Junior to come pick me up. I find an unopened bill on Jax's counter with his address, so I text it to Junior. Not even a minute goes by, and he replies that he's on his way.

Jax walks toward me with a cute smirk. Little does he know, his night's about to do a complete 180. I'm not mad that he's messing with Jessica; I'm clear on the fact that we aren't exclusive, but the fact that he brought me into her workplace to meet her on *our* date is pretty disgusting. Even if they weren't fucking at that point, it's pretty clear now that he was interested in fucking her.

I must have "disgust" written all over my face, because his smirk quickly turns into confusion. "Is everything okay?" he asks.

"No, everything is not okay. You need to quickly get your ducks in a row, because shit is about to hit the fan," I break it to him. His forehead wrinkles as he tries to decode this. Let me make it more simple for him. "Jessica, the girl you must have fucked the other night, is on her way over here. I was grabbing your sponge and happened to notice the text that came scrolling across your phone. You probably have about five minutes to come up with something *really* good to tell her, or you're going to have a major fucking breakdown on your hands. Let me guess— you didn't mention to her that you were dating other people?" I question, now leaning against his counter with my arms folded over my chest.

He runs his hand through his perfectly gelled hair. This is when you know a man is panicking. "You're joking with me, right?" he questions. He picks up his phone and reads through the text. Not even a minute goes by and the doorbell rings. "Shit! Fuck!" he screams.

I'm a little taken aback. This is a totally new side I'm seeing. The doorbell rings again. "Um, she's not going to leave. You better go answer it," I tell him.

He looks to me, then looks to the door, then back at me. "Listen, Kinsey, I'm so sorry. But she's freaking nuts! I swear, I've never done anything but take her out for some drinks. She's gotten all stalkerish on me, and I can't get rid of her," he informs me, trying to cover his tracks. Unfortunately, he's talking to a woman with much experience in this department. Women usually don't go crazy unless they've been lead on.

"Save it, Jax!" I walk over to the door and buzz her in. He completely flips his lid. I just open the door, lean against the wall, and cross my arms while waiting for this shit show to start.

Jessica comes bolting through the door. She takes one look at me, and then she goes off. I get a text from Junior that he's outside, asking if he needs to come up. I quickly text him no, and I slide out the door. Neither of them notice, and that's fine with me. I'm ready to go home.

CHAPTER FOURTEEN

Junior

As soon as I received Kinsey's text, I left. I swear, if that dickhead touched her or hurt her in any way, he's going to see a side of me that I haven't even seen before. I pull up to the building and text her to see if she needs me to come up. She texts back no.

Another minute goes by, then I see her exiting the elevators through the glass doors. I can now breathe. She looks irritated and pissed as she walks toward my car.

She opens the door and plops in. I look her over quickly before pulling off. "Are you okay? Did he hurt you?" I question, a little desperate to know the answers.

"That was a fucking shit show! No, I'm fine, Junior. Thanks for coming," she tells me. I pull off. "But let me tell you—his ass is probably dead by now."

"What do you mean? What happened in there?"

"Let's just say you were right. And yes, I am admitting this. So don't take it to your head. He was sleeping with Jessica, and she went into Beth-stalker-mode on him. I saw her text while Jax was in the bathroom. She asked if he was with me, and since he didn't respond, she showed up. It was a mess! Thank God you came fast, because I wasn't about to sit there and witness his murder," she explains with a laugh.

I'm glad she finds this humorous instead of devastating. "Wow, that *is* crazy. I knew he was a douche. Guys know these kind of things—"

Before I can finish, she interrupts. "Oh, so is this the part where you tell me, 'I told you so?'"

"No, Kins. This is the part where I ask if you are okay. So are you okay?"

She looks out her passenger window, probably so I can't see her face. "Yeah, I'm okay. I'm just glad this happened now before I wasted anymore of my time," she finishes.

"Me too. I'm glad you finally got to see his true colors."

She turns to look at me. "What do you mean by that?"

Shit! Me and my dumb mouth. "Um, just that you got to see what I saw finally."

She furrows her brows and squints her eyes. "No, I think you are referring to something else. Do you know something that I don't?"

I take a deep breath and just say it. I tell her about Jonas and what he told me. Then I tell her the conversation between Jax and I before they left. She just listens, taking it all in.

"Kins? Say something."

She stays silent. I pull into the garage and park. She immediately exits the car and starts walking toward the elevator. The ride up to the apartment is tense and quiet. As soon as I close the apartment door behind me, I ask if she's upset with me.

She turns to me. "Are you fucking kidding me, Junior? Why didn't you say something? What the hell kind of friend are you?" she yells. Damn, she is really upset.

"Kins, I'm sorry. I should have told you, but I thought you might not have believed me," I admit. I follow her into the kitchen. "I thought you would think I was just jealous, and I wanted you to see for yourself what a prick this guy is."

She grabs a wineglass from the cupboard and pours a huge glass for herself. "Go fuck yourself, Junior!" She walks to her room, leaving me standing alone.

Damn, she is pissed. I've never seen her this upset, let alone at me. I royally screwed this one up. Here Jax is, playing her like a fiddle, and I get the heat for it. How is this even fair? I want to rush into her room to ask her this, but I stop myself. She needs some time to cool down, and I'm exhausted from all this mindfucking.

"Hey, bro!" Jeff greets. I slap him up. I nod my head to Kyle. I'm a member at LA Fitness, but Jeff suggested I meet them here, at Pumps Gym, instead. Working out with someone to pass the time is much better than going solo, so I agreed. "Man, you look like shit. You and Kinsey have a long night?" Jeff inquires with a wink.

I shake my head. This guy's always trying to catch me slipping up. "No, man. She got mad at me and refused to talk to me the rest of the night," I reply.

"Damn, I wouldn't want to be on the receiving end of her madness. I can only imagine that she grows horns and fire spits out of her mouth when she's pissed," Jeff jokes.

We all laugh. "So, what did she get mad about?" Kyle asks between presses.

I jump on the treadmill to warm up. "She's been seeing this guy Jax, and—"

"Whoa, whoa, wait—what are you talking about? You two have been hanging out a lot, right?" Jeff asks, interrupting me.

"Yeah, but she made it very clear to me in the beginning that she's not interested in anything serious. She was seeing him before we started hanging out more, so what was I supposed to do? We aren't dating. If I told her to stop seeing him, she would have backed off from me, and that would have been it for any type of friendship," I explain.

"So, what was she mad about?" Kyle questions again.

"She was pissed because Jonas told me he sees Jax at the bar all the time leaving with that blonde bartender, Jessica. She found this out directly from Jax last night, and when I told her I already knew, she flipped out. She told me to fuck off, and I haven't talked to her since."

Kyle whistles and sits up from the bench. "Bro," he says, shaking his head. "You either have to be upfront with stuff like that, or you have to keep it in the hidden vault forever. You never admit to a woman that you've been keeping things from her, because then she's going to wonder what else you've been keeping from her," he informs me, breaking it down. Normally, I wouldn't listen to his advice, but he kind of has experience in this department.

"Yeah, man. You're never supposed to admit those things. Kyle's right; take it to the grave or tell her right away. Women are very good at holding grudges and using this sort of stuff as weapons against you later—believe me!" Jeff agrees.

"Okay, okay, now what do I do? How do I fix this?" I ask the both of them. This is crazy. I'm older and they were the male town whores growing up, and here I am asking them for relationship advice.

Kyle lies back down to continue his chest reps. "You go home, and you apologize for not telling her right away."

Jeff jumps in. "Yeah, good luck with her, man. She's going to make you work for this one. She's evil like that."

"Great. Thanks, guys."

When I get home, Kinsey is gone. Perfect. I just wanted to get this groveling over with. I jump into the shower quickly and then lie down on my bed until she comes home. I have no idea what I'm going to say, so I guess I'm going to wing it. I'm not sure if this is the best idea, but it's the only idea I have.

I'm groggy when I crack my eyes open, and the room is dark. Shit! I must have fallen asleep. I look over at my phone, and it says quarter to five. Kinsey has to be home by now. I get up, wash my face, and head out of my room.

  The apartment is quiet and dark, but I hear the TV on in Kinsey's room—she's home. My heart palpitates hard and fast through my chest as I stand at her door. I bring my hand up to knock but stop. I have to calm myself before I look like an ass when I go in there. I'm too nervous. What if she doesn't want to see me? What if she tells me what we have is over with? How will I be able to move on? I'm not ready to move on. She's got a hold on me somehow. This whole thing is just crazy. I don't even know how I got to this point, but she's become entwined in my thoughts and branded on every inch of my soul.

  This is it. I have to man up. You got this, Junior. You got this. I knock on her door. I hear bare footsteps on the hardwood floor. The doorknob twists, the door opens, and she stands in front of me. My mouth goes dry, and I feel like I've been drained of all my words.

  "What do you want, Junior?"

  I swallow hard. "Can we talk?"

  She turns her back to me and walks toward her bed. At least she's giving me a chance to speak instead of slamming the door in my face. I probably have, at the most, five minutes to speak my case.

She sits down on her bed and faces me, clearly uninterested in what I have to say. Well here goes nothing. "Listen, I'm sorry I didn't tell you about Jax sooner. I should have, and I was wrong for keeping it from you," I admit to her. I was instructed not to mention any reasons why I did what I did, because she'll just see it as a lame excuse. "I promise; it won't happen again. Can you forgive me?"

I stand here, switching my weight from feet to feet like a nervous asshole, waiting for her to speak. The wheels are turning as she contemplates her next response.

She takes a breath. "Junior, you fucked up. You kept something from me, and I thought we were on this honesty policy. You let me down. I swear, if you do it again, I'm going to rip your balls off and feed them to you. Got it?"

Damn, she always takes things to the next level with her ruthless mouth, but I'm beginning to love that mouth. Yes, I said it. I think I'm falling in love with this girl. I've never been in love before, but the moment I thought we were over, my whole world felt as though it was tumbling down. And now that I'm standing in front of her, begging for her to forgive me, I realize she is it for me. She completes me. I never want to lose her, and I'm never going to let her slip between my fingers again.

I crack a smile. This is her giving me a second chance. She has to feel something for me, or she would have just told me to fuck off. "Got it!" I reply.

I walk toward her, dying to touch her. I haven't touched her in over twenty-four hours. I'm having Kinsey withdrawal.

She shakes her head. "Oh, no! This doesn't mean you get to come over here and grope me. You stay over there Mr. Fancy Pants!" I hear her, but I know she doesn't mean it. She's just being a hard-ass.

I continue to stalk her and then pounce on top of her, tickling the crap out of her. I just need to cut the tension between us. She giggles—I love the sound of it— and we wrestle until she is on top, straddling me.

Things come to a halt as we stop and lock eyes

with each other. The fun and games ignite into an intense, burning fire of desire. All I want to do is be buried deep inside of her. I grab her neck and bring her down to me. She follows without hesitation. She nips at my bottom lip, and it sends a jolt straight down to my cock.

I want to taste her. "Sit on my face," I tell her. She pauses, unsure for a moment, but I pull down her shorts and grab her hips to direct her over me. I dig in. She's magnificent and perfect in every possible way. "You taste amazing," I say as I lick her and tease her until she is screaming above me.

I guide her back down to me. She lays her head on my chest to gather herself as she comes down from her orgasm. "Damn, I need to package that tongue and sell it to all the deprived women out there. We would make a fortune!" she jokes.

I laugh. "Oh yeah? Well you should test ride this dick then; I bet it won't disappoint! Maybe we can package this up too."

She lifts herself up and slowly sinks down on me. I think I've died and gone to heaven. My eyes roll back. She feels incredible—warm and tight. Every time feels like the first time with her. How did I get so lucky? She moves over me in a graceful, seductive rhythm. I grab hold of her hips, digging my fingers into her skin and enjoying the ride. I allow her to take full control.

Each little moan of hers brings me closer to my release. She bites her bottom lip and throws her head back as she begins to unravel. I can't hold back any longer; I'm a goner as soon as she yells out that she's coming.

She lies on top of me, breathless and spent. She has sucked the energy right out from me. "Damn, Kins, you're like the Energizer Bunny."

She giggles. "Your dick passed inspection; we can definitely sell it for top dollar!"

I roll her over so I am now in charge and kiss her as though the world's going to end. She just does it for me. I want to tell her this, but I know I will lose her for good, so I don't. I lay my head on her chest, close my eyes, and secretly pray that one day she will feel the same way.

I turn the shower on and wait for the steam to cloud up the bathroom. The door creaks open, and Kinsey pops through it. "Hey, sunshine. Why didn't you wake me?" she asks.

She looks pretty well-rested, considering. "You looked so peaceful. I didn't want to bother you," I tell her while taking off my boxer briefs. She licks her lips while taking a peek at my junk. I smirk and she grins. "Do you see something you like?" I ask.

Kinsey just rolls her eyes. "I'm out! I'm going to shower in my bathroom. If I stay in here, we won't get to work on time." She throws me the peace sign and leaves the bathroom. I shake my head and chuckle. She's straight crazy, and the craziest part is that she's growing on me. Everything about her seems to be growing on me. I don't know whether I'm turning batshit crazy from being around her so much or if it's these feelings that I'm starting to develop. Either way, I seem to be fucked.

I get my slacks on, tuck in my button-up shirt, and head out to the kitchen to grab some coffee. I am in dire need of it. Last night's escapades have left me a bit sluggish.

Kinsey pours me a cup. "Oooh, I'm really liking the purple on you! It complements you well. Most people end up looking like a huge grape or eggplant."

I pour my cream and sugar in and take a sip of the hot liquid—it tastes like heaven. "Geez, never really thought about it like that, but good to know for other colored shirts. I don't want to end up looking like an orange or cucumber in the future," I respond sarcastically.

She smacks me on my arm. I lean down and steal a kiss from her. "Oh, it's pizza and beer night, so no working late tonight!" she orders.

Damn, she's bossy. "O-kay, is this something new?"

"Yup!" she answers as she walks toward the door. "Let's put a move on it, sexy ass, before people start to wonder why we're late!"

I can't help but get turned on. She now has me sporting a chub. What the hell is this woman doing to me?

I am working through my lunch. Since I can't stay late tonight, I have to get everything done now. I look up to the knock on my door—it's my mother.

"Hey, Ma. What's up?"

She closes the door and takes a seat. Aww, man! Here it comes! What did I do now?

"Oh, I just noticed you and Kinsey have been driving in together. Have you two been getting along?" she asks. This is her roundabout way of asking if we're dating.

"Yes, we have. I mean, we do have the same friends, and we do live together, so us getting along was bound to happen," I answer.

She smiles, but I can see she is trying to decide whether to keep her mouth shut or not. "And what happened with Bridgette? She told me you asked her out to dinner last week—"

God, she is not going to stop until I throw her a bone. "Yes, I did. We had dinner and that was it. She's not it for me, so I let her go. I have a thing going on with someone. We're just getting to know each other—trying to see where things go. It's nothing serious at the moment; we're just friends for now. So can you lay off me a bit?"

She takes a breath before she speaks. "Yes, you're right, dear. I just worry about you. You work so hard, and you just don't get to enjoy the fruits of your labor. I told Dad he should cut back on your workload so you can go have some fun and socialize more."

I throw my hands up in the air. "Mom! Come on! I am a grown man for Christ's sake! If I feel I need to cut back on my hours, I will talk to Dad myself. Geez, you are too much sometimes!"

She gets up and comes around my desk to give me a kiss on the cheek. "I just want the best for my boys; is that so much to ask? Oh, and just so you know, I'm secretly cheering for Kinsey," she admits before leaving my office.

I bang my head on my desk dramatically.

"What's going on, bro?"

I look up, and it's Jeff in my office now.

"My mother is what's up. She's up to no good," I inform him.

Jeff laughs. "So, I guess it's pizza and beer night at

your house now?" he asks.

"Kinsey invited you guys?"

"Yeah, Kinsey spoke with Elise. What's up with this anyways? Since when do you guys throw couples things?" he questions.

I was waiting for this. Now, do I tell him the truth or leave it between Kinsey and I? "Kinsey and I have been hanging out some. We figured since we live together, maybe it was time we got to know each other," I tell him.

His smile turns into a huge shit-eating grin. "Well, well, you've finally broken down and fucked her! My man!" Jeff congratulates.

I begin to shake my head, but before I can open my mouth, he stops me. "Dude, don't even try to lie. I can see it written all over your face—you're all sparkling and shit. She must have really gave it to you good, and honestly, all I can say is that it's about damn time!"

What the hell am I supposed to say to that? "Okay, okay, we've been hooking up, but can we just keep this between us? I'm kind of liking what's going on, and I don't want it getting ruined over me opening my mouth to you, okay?"

"You got it, bro. My lips are sealed," he agrees.

Good, now I hope she didn't invite my brother over. "What about Kyle?"

Jeff snickers. "Dude, you guys just really need to get over your shit. It's just getting ridiculous now. But no, I don't think they will be there. Oh, and Julian wanted to get together Sunday for some guy time. You game?"

"Yeah, I think I can manage. So, did you and Elise come up with a wedding date yet?"

He blows out a big breath. This looks serious. "She's not ready to set a date. It's her mom; she wants to wait until she's been sober for awhile and is on her feet before we start planning. Sometimes I feel so helpless. Her mother's issues are so out of my control, and I hate it, man."

"Damn, man. That's got to be tough. Elise is a strong chick, and you are doing everything you need to be doing for her and more. These issues with her mom will never completely go away. Once an addict, you're an addict forever. But that also doesn't mean you guys should put your lives on hold either," I tell him.

Man, this is some heavy crap to be dealing with this morning. If this is an indication of what the rest of the day will be like, I might need a beer.

"That's what I've been telling her. I guess we just have to take it one day at a time. So listen, you need us to bring anything? Elise makes some banging-ass chicken wing dip. I know Kins loves that crap—"

"Yeah, bring it."

Jeff gets up to leave but has one last thing to say. "I have to admit, even though Kins is one crazy chick, I'm kind of digging the idea of you two together," he confesses.

Oh, I've got another fan on my hands. I just wave him off. I get up and shut my door. I really need to get some work done. Hopefully this eliminates the traffic in my office.

I look at my phone to see the time—I keep a Post-it note over my computer's clock to keep me from looking at it every two seconds—and it's now four-thirty. Only thirty more minutes, and I can finally have that beer I've been craving. My lower back aches, and my ass is numb from sitting so long today.

I send out my last email right before I hear a knock on the door. I look up, and Bridgette is standing in front of me.

"Hey, Bridgette. What can I do for you?"

She puts a folder on my desk. "Your father wanted me to bring you over the Jameson file. I finished the edits on his memoir, and I emailed them to you. Look over the edits and tell me what you think. I have a phone conference with him tomorrow, so if you have anything you would like to add, I can relay the message or you can join in on the conference."

Wow, it feels good to get back to business with her. I was afraid this would never happen. "Okay, let me look this over and get back to you. What time's the conference?"

She fidgets with her necklace. "Ten."

I scroll through the file quickly. "Okay, how about we meet in here to discuss everything at nine-thirty tomorrow?"

She looks a little unsure. "Um, okay," she agrees before heading toward the door.

"And thanks for bringing this over," I say loudly. She just smiles before she leaves.

I shut down everything a little early and head over to Kinsey's office. Unfortunately, Kyle is sitting in there with her. I almost want to turn around, but she sees me and waves me in. Shit!

"I was just coming to see if you're almost ready to head out?" I ask Kinsey. I'm secretly praying she doesn't say anything about tonight to Kyle. I wouldn't mind if Max brought Penelope, but that automatically includes my brother in on the invite.

"Yeah, can you give me five? I'll meet you out at the car," she responds.

I nod and leave quickly.

After about ten minutes, Kinsey finally makes an appearance.

She jumps in the car. "Hey, you ready? We need to stop and grab the beer."

"Yeah, I'm ready. So, what time are Jeff and Elise coming by?" I ask.

"I told them about six so we can have some time to

get changed and relax a bit. Are you bothered that I asked them to come?"

I was looking forward to spending the night with just her, but I don't want to make her feel bad. "No, not at all," I fib. I pull into the gas station. "What kind of beer do you girls want to drink?"

"Um, grab us some Coronas."

Before I exit the car, I reach over for a kiss. I'm expecting her to back away, but she immediately responds to me, and I am loving it.

I grab two twelve-packs and head out.

We get to the apartment and both head to our own rooms to change. Sleeping with your roommate is the weirdest thing. We both have our own personal space, which is good for the moments we need alone, but now what? Do we sleep together every single night or just the nights we have sex? Do we make plans every night after work, or do we still do our own thing? She mentioned Jax the other night, so I guess my next question to her should be—are we still dating other people?

This is what we discussed the other week, but I feel

things have changed a bit. I just wonder how she feels about the whole situation. I almost feel it's too soon to ask these questions, but I hate doubt and being left in the dark. If anything between us is going to work, including friendship, we need to be open and honest with each other.

I hear her on the phone ordering pizza as I walk into the kitchen. She's wearing some tight sweatpants and a black tank top—still showing off her curves. I guess even she gets a little conservative when there's company involved. I smile at the fact that she enjoys wearing her tiny shorts and see-through tank top for me only. The thought of another man seeing her like that upsets me.

I sneak up behind her, wrap my arms around her waist, and apply tiny kisses to her neck while she's on the phone. She squirms and then turns around to give me the evil eye. As soon as she hangs up, she elbows me in the chest. I grunt.

"Damn, woman! You have one sharp elbow!" I whine.

"You're lucky it's only your gut I hit," she jokes, closing the gap between us for a kiss. My cock immediately gets hard, poking her in the stomach.

She looks down and laughs. "Wow, with just a kiss? Is that all it takes?" she wonders.

"I can't help it. You turn me on," I shrug.

She giggles. "Why Mr. Saunders, have you turned into every other man on the planet? I thought you were different," she teases.

Her phone dings, alerting her of a new text. She leaves my side to look. The crease between her brows appears as she reads the text.

"Is everything okay?" I ask.

She replies quickly, then puts the phone down. "Yes, sorry. It was just Jax. He's apologizing and wants to see me," she states calmly. Is this guy serious? He definitely has some balls.

My blood begins to simmer. "Are you going to see him?"

She grabs two beer bottles out of the refrigerator, opens both, and hands me one. I take a nice, long pull. "I told him I was unsure if I am going to have time."

Fuck! "Damn, Kins. Am I supposed to be okay

with you seeing him?" Maybe I shouldn't go here with her yet, but fuck it. I don't care.

She puts her hand on her hip. "What do you mean by that? I thought we agreed on this subject already. I told you I would still be dating other people, and I'm not looking to settle down. I want to hear him out."

I take another long sip of my beer. "Yes, that was before I was having sex with you almost every day. I don't want another man's hands on you. The thought makes me sick! You shouldn't want anything to do with that douche anyways. I can't believe you're even considering it!"

She stops a moment to digest what I've just said, but before she can reply, the door buzzes. Damn. I'm not ready for this conversation to end.

She walks toward the intercom. "We can finish this conversation tonight when everyone leaves," she tells me. Great. Yeah, that sounds like some fun. By then, I won't be interested in talking unless it's asking her which sexual position she wants.

She buzzes Jeff and Elise in. I can already feel the tension building between us. Elise walks in with the dip, and Kinsey goes crazy. Jeff comes in with another twelve-pack. You would think we were throwing a party or something. Then the buzzer goes off again. I look to Kinsey, and she shrugs her shoulders and walks to the door.

A minute later, I hear a baby screech, and I know exactly who it is. Damn her! I feel so guilty thinking this way, because I don't see my niece as much as I should, but I wanted to relax and enjoy the night, not look at Kyle's face all night.

Kinsey walks over to greet them and then walks by me to grab her beer. "You better be on your best behavior," she whispers as she walks by. Is this chick out of her mind?

As soon as Penelope sees me, she starts wiggling in Max's arms, reaching for me. "She loves her Uncle Junior!" Max says, laughing.

Penelope practically jumps into my arms, and the whole room sighs. I give her a tight squeeze and a kiss on the cheek, and she giggles. Her laugh is so contagious. It makes the whole room follow suit.

Kyle nods and slaps me on the back before walking to the refrigerator to grab a beer. I sit Penelope down on the counter but make sure I have a tight grip on her.

"Dude, when's the pizza get here? I am starving!" Jeff yells.

"I just ordered it like ten minutes ago. Eat some damn dip," Kinsey replies.

Jeff whips his head back. "Damn, Kins, is that any way to treat your guest?" he replies sarcastically.

"Blow me," she says back.

Max steps in between them. "Okay you two, enough! And watch the language. Penelope will begin to pick things up real soon. I don't need her first words to be 'blow me.'" I can't help but laugh.

Kinsey laughs along with me. "Yes, you are right. I need to learn to control my big bad mouth, or my goddaughter will be one small human with one large sailor's vocabulary!"

Max goes into the living room and breaks out the Pack 'n Play. She feels like the crawling stage will be on the horizon real soon, so it's important to keep Penelope contained, especially in a non-baby-proof house. I bring my niece over and set her down in the playpen amongst her toys.

I overhear Elise talking to Kinsey about her vacation coming up. It's only a reminder of how boring and quiet this place is going to be without her.

"You really like her, don't you?" Max asks.

I must have been staring in Kinsey's direction without even realizing it. I'm just drawn to her, and I can't help it. "Man, Max, I think I do. She's just growing on me at a rapid speed. I can't take a moment to breathe, because she seems to be in every breath I take. I no longer find myself annoyed by her—more like intrigued. I think I was blocking her before, because I knew deep down inside if I let her in, I would be a goner. Now look at me."

Max laughs but then gets serious. "You're a man that likes a girl. There's nothing wrong with that, Junior. To be honest, I think it goes both ways. You're just going to have to be patient with her. Kinsey is a huge pain in the ass, and when she has her mind made up, it sometimes takes heaven and earth to move before she realizes her decisions are wrong. She'll come around. Just don't give up," Max advises.

"Did she tell you what has been going on lately?" I question.

Penelope screeches to get my attention. I lean over the playpen to tickle her. "You mean, about you two doing the dirty deed?" I chuckle. "Yeah, she told me," Max comes clean.

Shit. "Does Kyle know?"

"Yes, she mentioned it to Kyle last night," she answers.

Well now I don't feel so bad opening my mouth to Jeff. I can only assume that Elise knows now, too.

"Listen, we are all supportive of you two. Hell, we've been dying for it to happen! If anyone's good for you, it's her. She gives you the pizzazz you're missing in your life. Look at you—you look happy for once. And you calm her and give her that balance she needs. Just whatever you do, don't give up," Max finishes.

The door buzzes, which means it's time to eat! We stuff our faces with pizza, then us guys head into the living room. The girls take Penelope into Kinsey's room, and then I watch as Jeff slowly heads there as well. Great. It's just

Kyle and I. if I didn't know any better, I would think this was a setup.

I take a sip of my beer, then look over at him doing the same. We sit in silence for a moment before Kyle finally speaks up.

"Listen, Junior. We need to talk. We need to fix whatever it is that's broken between us. If not for our friends, then for my daughter and our parents. I don't know at what point you started hating me, but I would like to know how to move past it," Kyle explains.

"It can't be fixed, because we can't change the past," I state. This kid is out of his freaking mind. I've had to clean up his damn mess more than once growing up, and he thinks it can all just be erased like it never happened.

"No shit, Sherlock!" he says, raising his voice. "Don't you think I know that? How about you tell me what the fuck I did wrong? What, did I beat you in too many races? Did Mom and Dad pay attention to me more growing up? Is that why you fucking hate me so damn much?" he screams.

I stand up. "Yes, all of that and more! But you

know what solidified it? Do you really want to know, Kyle?" I scream back.

"Yes! Fucking just tell me!"

"It was because of Mary!" I admit.

Kyle just huffs like I am pathetic. "Are you serious, bro? You're still upset about that chick?"

I'm about to lose it. "That fucking *chick* was pregnant with your damn baby, Kyle! When she came to you to tell you, you dumped her like she was just another girl on your list. You were done with her, so you threw her away. That night, she went home and downed a bottle of pills. *I* was the person she called last! And *I* was the person who called the ambulance, raced to her house, and rode with her all the way to the hospital. She almost died, you know!" I yell to him.

He just shakes his head and sits back down. Yeah, exactly what I thought he would do. Back down like a coward. "She lost the baby, and it crushed her. She was never the same after that. She was never the same after *you*, but you got to go on living like nothing had changed. If you would have just taken a moment to listen to her, a moment to care, it all could have been prevented," I finish, a little calmer this time.

He has his head in his hands. "Shit! How could you have kept this from me this long? Why didn't you ever tell me?" he asks.

"Would it have mattered?"

He looks up at me with anger. "Of course it would have mattered! I wasn't that heartless! Yes, I was an egotistical, selfish asshole, but I was still a fucking kid! People change, you know. You can't hold that against me forever. You never even gave me the chance to react. Have you spoken to her since?"

I sit back down. "Not for a couple of years. She sort of fell off the grid. I tried reaching out to her parents, but they told me to move on with my life—whatever that meant."

"Does Mom or Dad know?" Kyle questions, a little worried.

"Nah, I didn't tell them either."

Just seeing Kyle's reaction makes me wonder if keeping this from him all these years was the right thing to do. Maybe I should have given him the benefit of the doubt, but I was just so upset with him, and I didn't want him to possibly make anything worse for Mary.

"Well, thank you for finally telling me. You know, I'm really serious about building some kind of relationship with you. Maybe we can't forget about the past, but I'm hoping we can forgive each other and start fresh from here on out," Kyle states.

This is going to be a hard move for me, but what's the harm in it? He is my blood. I watch Jeff and his brother, Julian, together and it pains me to know I could have that but have chosen not to all these years. My parents are in constant turmoil over the rift between my brother and I, so maybe it is time to put a bandage over it and let it heal.

I nod. "Yeah, man. It's going to take some time, but I'm in."

We both stand up and slap each other up with a quick hug. I think this is the first time I've hugged my brother in over ten years. I have to admit, it feels good. Kyle yells to the others to come on out. I'm sure they've been listening with their ears to the door this whole time anyways.

The door opens and everyone files out. They look a little nervous.

"Hey, there's no blood. You guys didn't kill each other. That's a good sign, right?" Jeff jokes.

Kyle laughs. "Yeah, man. We're good. No blood spilled," he replies.

The rest of the night was actually pretty enjoyable. We played some Yahtzee once Penelope fell asleep and drank lots of beers. I'm pretty buzzed. We say goodbye to everyone, and its now just Kinsey and me.

She stands near the door, and I'm in the kitchen. I see her take a deep breath before she walks toward me. I know we need to finish the conversation that was interrupted; I'm just not so sure I want to do it now.

"So, where did we leave off?" she asks.

Damn, talk about jumping right into it. "I think we left off with you seeing Jax."

"Listen, Junior, we talked about all of this last week and came to an agreement," she starts. Before I let her finish the rest, I rush toward her and grab her face—not giving her any time to react—and smash my lips to hers. Fuck this conversation. We can hash this out tomorrow. I just want to feel every part of her body against my skin.

Just the sight of her has me hard as a rock. All I want to do is bury myself deep inside of her right now. She struggles for a moment, then gives up. This makes me a very happy man. I lift her onto the kitchen counter to begin my assault on her. I want her screaming my name and withering under my control.

There's very rare moments where she allows me to lead, but when it happens, it makes me want to give her the world. I just wish I would have given in to my desires a lot earlier. I can't get enough of her now.

"I can't get enough of you," I tell her. She kisses me deeper, digging her nails into my back. I rip her sweatpants and panties off, and drop to my knees so I can taste her. It gives me pleasure to see her spread eagle and vulnerable in front of me. She's the most beautiful thing I've ever laid eyes on. How am I ever going to get her out of my head?

I swipe my tongue over her clit, nipping then

teasing her. I run my finger around her drenched opening, then dip one finger in to coat it with her slick juices while I continue to massage her swollen clit with my tongue. I want to try something new, so I slide my now-lubed finger down south to her asshole, and slowly enter it inside her. She gasps and I stop. "Does that hurt?" I ask. She shakes her head and urges me to continue.

I lick every inch of her, stopping only to fuck her pussy with my tongue while still fingering her tight asshole. I wonder how good it would feel to fuck that tight ass. She wiggles and moans. I hold her hips in place while I assault her clit with my tongue over and over until she cums hard as hell. She tastes amazing.

She's breathless. "Holy fuck! That felt unbelievable, Junior!"

I wrap her legs around me and take her to my bed. Everything else can wait; tonight I just want to get lost in her.

CHAPTER FIFTEEN

Kinsey

My head is pounding like I just got hit in the head with a boulder. What the hell? Where am I? I look over and Junior is snuggled up next to me. Shit! How did I end up in Junior's bed again? Oh, yes. A flash of heat runs through my body. I know exactly how I got here.

I slowly sit up, so my head doesn't explode, and slide out of bed. I'm in major need of Advil. I drank way too many beers last night, and I have to be to work in less than three hours. This isn't good.

I chase the pills with water and head back to bed. I begin walking through my door, but I see my cold, empty bed. I look back down the hall to Junior's room where it's nice and warm. I can't believe I'm doing this, but I slip back into bed with him. I feel comfort and secure with him lying beside me. Weird.

I fall back asleep until his alarm blares loudly. Geez, I almost thought someone was in here with a bullhorn. My head is no longer pounding, but I'm still exhausted. From the looks of Junior, he seems in pretty bad shape as well. He groans and rolls over, holding his head.

I sit up and shake him gently. "Do you need some Advil?" I ask. He nods his head. I get out of bed and head to the kitchen for the pills and water.

I bring it back and sit beside him. "Here. Drink all the water too. It will help. Do you think you can work?" he shakes his head and rolls back over.

I text Max that we are both taking a personal day. I think I've only used one other this year, so I'm due for it. I lie back down next to Junior and close my eyes.

"Hey, Kins. Get up. It's almost one o'clock," Junior whispers in my ear. My eyes snap open. What the fuck? I never sleep this late. My whole entire morning has been wasted by sleep. "Hey, sleepyhead. We slept a long time. I guess we better chill out on the beers next time," Junior jokes.

I feel like a hot mess. I can only imagine what I

look like, and let's not even talk about my ungodly breath! I cover my mouth before I talk. "I can't believe we slept this long. I need to go freshen up," I tell him before jumping out of bed.

He laughs. "Yeah, me too."

I grab my clean clothes and head into the bathroom to jump in for a quick shower. I can smell Junior all over me, then it hits me—Junior is everywhere, pretty much consuming my whole life these past couple of days. Last night's argument about Jax also hits me like a ton of bricks, and I can't breathe. I try to breathe in through my mouth to suck in more oxygen, but I can't inhale it fast enough. All the air is being sucked out of me. I grab my chest as I struggle for air. I put one hand against the shower wall to hold myself up before I pass out.

I see little specks of black dots fading in and out, and I know at this point if I don't sit down, I'm done. I slide down the wall and yank my legs to my chest. The hot water beats down on me as I concentrate on breathing. After another five minutes or so, the panic attack finally subsides. This is all beginning to be too much. I'm enjoying his company way too much, too. I keep drawing the lines and then blurring them up.

But how do I tell him without hurting his feelings that we should back up and slow down? And since when do I give a damn about his feelings? Damn him! I think I want to tell him to back off, but deep down, I'm not quite sure if that's what I really want.

I get out of the shower and dry off. I throw my hair into a messy bun and head to my room to change. I smell coffee and bacon. My stomach growls with hunger. I follow the tantalizing aroma to the kitchen, and Junior is at the stove, flipping the bacon.

"Here," he hands me my coffee. "Have a seat. Breakfast is almost done."

I take a sip of my coffee and close my eyes, enjoying the flavor as it slides down my throat. Heaven in a cup. "Junior, how's that head of yours?" I ask.

"Almost as good as new. I just need some food in my system. You kind of wore me out last night," he tells me.

He dishes out our plates, hands me mine, and

comes around the counter to sit next to me. I keep thinking about last night and how we never finished our conversation. I really need to just come out and say it.

"Junior, I'm not going to stop seeing Jax just because you're feeling insecure. I like him and I like you. This is what 'dating' is all about. I didn't throw a fit when you were seeing Bridgette," I say, but before I can go any further, he jumps in.

"Hold on—you may not have thrown a fit, but you made sure she knew you were around. You made yourself very present, especially at The Tavern—enough for her to ask about us," he advises me. "And just for the record, I am *not* insecure. I just don't like sharing, and I sure as hell don't want him kissing the lips that I have been kissing!"

I roll my eyes. "I'm not your property, you know. I can kiss whoever the hell I want to. And if I messed anything up between you and Bridgette, I'm sorry," I inform him, not looking for a response. I take another sip of my coffee and finish up my eggs, then I turn back to him. "What is it you want from me, Junior?" I question, patiently waiting for his response.

I hear him huff like a little kid. I almost want to laugh, but I'm trying to keep things serious here. "I don't know, Kins. I like you. I like you a lot. God, I never thought I would ever be saying this, but you're growing on me. I wish you would just let your guard down and give us a real chance."

"You mean, make us exclusive? Do you really think that's the best idea since we live together?" I wonder.

"What's the difference?"

"The difference is my freedom. I don't have to answer to anyone, nor do I have to worry about getting my heart ripped into pieces. What you're asking for is too messy, too complicated. I'm not ready for complicated yet." I finish up my coffee and walk around to put my dishes in the sink.

"Fine. You win for now, but I'm not giving up. Will you still be seeing Jax?"

"I'm not sure. Why, is that a problem if I do?" I wonder. I like making his ass squirm; he sure made mine squirm last night. To be honest, Jax made a dick move with Jessica. My feelings aren't hurt, but I don't like seeing another girl being taken advantage of. He wasn't honest with her, and that's what I have the problem with. Makes me wonder what he may be keeping from me.

"I just want to make sure I will be around next time you see him. I don't like it one bit, but I'll be here if you need me," he replies, taking a sip of his orange juice.

I feel the tension rolling off of him. It's filling the air in between us, but I've been very clear with him from the beginning what this is—just friends with benefits. Nothing more, nothing less.

I get a text from Max as I head to my room. I need a moment alone right now.

"Hey, chick! Are you feeling any better?" she asks.

"Yeah, just clearing some things up with Junior," I respond.

I turn on my TV.

"Ut oh, what happened?"

"He wants to be exclusive. I don't," I text.

There's a pause between this text. It must be a long one. "Kins, you should give him a chance. He really likes you. He actually really adores you. I knew he would once he got to know you, and here he is, trying to open up to you, and you're shutting him down. If you don't feel the same way as he does, then you need to let him go."

Damn, I know she's right, but I don't want to. As much as he doesn't want me to be with anyone else, I feel the same about him. There's just no way I'm admitting this to anyone!

"But he's *so* good in bed!" I add with a pouty-face emoji.

"Girl, if he's anything like his brother, then I feel ya!" I wrinkle my nose at this thought. Kyle's hot, but picturing him that way is just so wrong.

"OMG. I'm done. Way too much info! I'm out! Deuces!" I text, with the emoji peace sign.

She texts back, "Lol!"

I throw the phone down on my bed. I just need to clear my mind for one moment. I don't want to think about anything or anyone; I just want to be. I can't wait to spend some time with my parents. I need my mother. I've never gone this long without seeing them. My mother's been wanting to come up here for a visit, but it's too hard for her to close the shop for that long.

She's a do-it-yourself type of person, so she only has one other person working for her. My father's always on her case about working too much. He wants her to hire more staff so she can enjoy life a bit more, but my mother wouldn't have it any other way.

My father's such a gentleman, and he adores my mother like no other. He still gets the twinkle in his eyes when he looks at her. I always loved watching them together. I always thought that I would have that type of love, until my world was crushed by Tommy. After that, my heart turned to stone.

How do I trust again? I'm sick of being alone, but I don't think I could survive another heartbreak. Junior's everything that I never thought he could be, and it scares the shit out of me. I'm just not ready to let go and jump yet. I don't know if I'll ever be ready.

I hear a knock on my door.

"Come in," I yell.

Junior walks in. "Hey, I'm going to the grocery store. Do you need anything?"

"Um, yeah, some tampons. The Pearl, regular-sized ones," I watch him squirm as he contemplates having to do this. His face turns pink, and he begins to stutter. "Oh my God! I was just joking, sweet cheeks! No, I'm good. I don't need anything, but thank you." I wink.

He looks overly relieved. "Okay, I'll be back in a bit."

I pull the covers over me and flip on Netflix. I'm going to make good use of playing hooky; it's called using my bed mileage points. I haven't had one of these lazy lounge days in pretty much for-never.

An hour goes by, then my phone rings. It's my mother. I put the phone on speaker, because I'm too lazy to hold it to my ear.

"Hey, Mama."

"Hey, sweetie. How's work going?" she asks.

"I'm home right now. I took the day off."

She gasps in shock. "*You* took a day off? I've been telling you to do that for years! Who is he? What's his name?" she interrogates. God, I forget she's my mother and knows me so damn well.

"Mom, he's just a friend. He's Kyle's brother, Junior. You know, my roommate," I tell her nonchalantly.

"Well, why don't you bring this friend with you when you come down here? I'm sure you could use the company while driving," she hints. I roll my eyes. "And don't roll your eyes at me!" Damn her! It's like she's some sort of witch or something.

I huff. "Mom, I'm not bringing him with me. He's just a friend, and he has a life of his own," I try to break it to her so she won't start hounding me. My mom hates that I've been alone this long. She wants me to have what she has with my dad, along with a million grandbabies.

"I'd be happy to go with you!" I turn and look at Junior like he has three heads. I'm going to beat him!

"Oh, goody! We are going to be so happy to have you here, Junior! I'll get your room ready for you, dear," she tells him. We can hear the excitement pouring from her words. She now speaks to me. "See, you didn't even have to ask! What a gentleman."

I slam my forearm over my face. "Mom, I'll talk to you later. I have to go," I lie, hanging up.

Junior is leaning against the door jamb, chuckling. "Oh, you are so going to get it!" I yell. I jump out of bed, and he backs up toward his room with his palms in the air.

I lunge at him but miss. I back him up all the way to the end of his bed; he has nowhere to go. Good.

"Okay, okay, relax. I thought I was just helping out. If you don't want me to come with you, then I won't," he says with the most adorable smirk. God, why does he have to look so cute and sexy right now?

I pounce on him, tackling him down to the bed. I hold his arms down above his head. "If you knew my mother, you wouldn't be saying this. She's going to hold you to this, even if she has to come up here and drive us both down herself."

He smiles. "So, I guess you're sort of stuck with me?"

I give him the bored, annoyed, I-don't-give-a-fuck face. "I guess I am stuck with you," I state, shrugging. I release his hands, trying to get off of him. He grabs my hips to hold me in place.

"Not so fast. I'm not done with you," he tells me. He runs his hands through my hair and brings my lips down to his. I'm a goner at this point. This alone convinces me to spend the rest of the afternoon locked away in his room.

CHAPTER SIXTEEN

Junior

Kinsey slept the whole night in my bed. I woke up this morning and just stared at her beautiful face for a while, memorizing every part of her before waking her up and hopping in the shower. Work today is going to be crazy-hectic, because of my day off. I've never once taken a day off from work, but honestly, I enjoyed playing a little hooky. The more time I spend with Kinsey, the more I see her as a permanent fixture in my life. I just wish I could get her to see this as well. I now have a whole week, just the two of us, to get her to fall for me. Yes, I said it—I want her to admit that these crazy, erratic, strong emotions I am feeling is what she is also feeling. If she would just let go, she would see what I see.

I dial my mother's extension. "Hey, honey."

"Mom, I need next week off. I'll be driving with Kinsey down to her parents," I tell her. I squeeze my eyes closed as I wait for the ear-deafening shriek from her.

"Oh, Junior, that's wonderful! Don't worry, I'll get everything covered for you on this end. So you guys are getting pretty serious, huh?"

"I'm just going down to keep her company on the road, Ma. I like Kinsey; I like her a lot. She's the complete opposite of me, but it keeps everything interesting," I tell her.

"Ahh, opposites do attract, you know."

"Yes, I see that now. She's a breath of fresh air," I say, then I hear a knock at my door. I turn in my chair, and Bridgette's standing here. I'm wondering how much of my conversation she overheard. "Mom, I gotta go," I say and hang up.

"Hey, Bridgette. What's going on?"

"I just wanted to go over the conference call that you missed yesterday."

Shoot! That totally slipped my mind. "Yes, right. Sorry, I wasn't feeling well yesterday. Come sit down." I point to the chair in front of my desk.

She sits down but seems a little guarded. "Kinsey

must have gotten the same bug?" she asks. I wasn't aware that was any of her business.

"I'm sorry, it's not really my place to speak for her. How did the conference with Mr. Jameson go?" I redirect her.

She flings her hair over her shoulders and sits up straight, as though she's squaring up with me. This is extremely awkward. "It went good. We went over all the edits. He just emailed me the corrections, and we can pass it along to the next step," she finishes.

"Okay, great. That's really good to hear."

She smiles proudly. "I have a video conference with L.G. Knight on Monday. Did you want to sit in on that one as well?"

"I can't. I'm actually leaving town for a week. But I can see if Kyle or Maxine would like to sit in. I will send them an email today along with the client's file so they will be well-informed before the video call," I advise her.

She looks a little disappointed. "Okay, either one of them will be fine. Are you going for business or pleasure?" she questions.

What is with all the personal questions? I know we went out to dinner one time, but that doesn't give her permission to grill me. "I'm just taking a week off for a little R&R," I tell her. At least it's the truth.

My phone rings. I look at the caller ID; it's Jeff. "Hey, this is an important call that I have to take," I say, holding up the phone. She nods and leaves. I wait until she is around the corner before speaking. "You totally just saved me!"

Jeff laughs. "I know. I walked by your office, and your face looked like you just diarrhea-ed all over yourself. Bridgette's been moping around ever since you and Kinsey both took off yesterday. I just hope she doesn't turn into Beth, bro."

I exhale and run my fingers through my hair. "Damn, I hope not. She was grilling me every chance she got. It was so uncomfortable."

"So I guess the girls are going out for dinner and some drinks. Kyle's on babysitting duty, so you wanna grab some beers and head over there after work with me?"

Kinsey hasn't mentioned this to me yet. "Yeah,

sounds good to me. Just FYI: it's not babysitting when it's your own kid," I inform him.

He laughs. "Yes, I guess you're right on that one!"

"Have you and Elise talked about having kids?" I ask him.

I hear nothing but crickets. I chuckle. "Yeah, we've talked about it here and there. But it's not on our agenda anytime soon. She wants to further her career here, and I want to take her to see the world, get her out of Rochester. She's never been anywhere outside of here."

"She wants to be an agent? Does Kyle know this?"

"Yes, he's been teaching her the ropes. He says she's catching on real fast, so the idea might not be that far off in the future. This gives her the confidence she needs. She's always so hard on herself, and I hate it."

"Well, good. I'm glad Kyle has taken her under his wing. She has all of us to help her," I tell him. "And you better give her the honeymoon of a lifetime. Contact Rose down at the travel agency; she'll totally hook you up."

His voice raises in excitement. "Yeah, man. I definitely will. I totally forgot she works there. Hey, I'm coming over." Jeff hangs up.

He comes in and takes a seat. "Hey, how was your day off with wackadoo? Did she sow your oats?" Jeff teases.

I lift my right eyebrow. "Watch it, man," I warn him. He snickers. "We had a relaxing day, but that's the only information you'll be getting. I never kiss and tell," I advise him.

Jeff laughs. Then Max comes strolling in. "Hey boys. Whatcha all laughing about?" she questions, looking between the both of us.

"Jeff, here, is trying to get the 411 on my day yesterday with Kinsey." I reply.

Max's face lights up. "Oh, yes! How was playing hooky? I have to say, that was definitely a shocker on both ends. My girl *never* takes off, even when she's sick. Just don't make it a habit. I'll come beat you; I need her," Max says with a smirk. She makes me nervous, because she will come looking for me.

"No worries. I promise," I tell her, giving her the scout's honor.

Jeff just snickers on the side. "Man, Junior, I feel bad for you. You have both of these crazies on your shit!" He can barely get it out before Max slaps him upside the head, and I throw my pen at his face.

"Ass!" Max says.

He gets up, backing up from Max. "I'm out before I have to claim workers' comp on your asses!"

I shake my head. I don't know how sweet Elise even deals with his ass.

Max takes a seat. Oh, man! Here we go.

"So give me the lowdown. Kins said you were going down to South Carolina with her?" I don't know if this is a statement or question.

I answer a quick email. "Yeah, I offered to drive down with her. She won't let her guard down. Every time I think I might be getting somewhere, I slam into her brick wall. I figure this way she has no choice but to spend time with me *without* distractions. I know she feels something for me. I just know. But she's too stubborn to admit it," I explain.

"Listen, Junior. My girl is as stubborn as they

come. It's going to take a lot for her to let go of the past, but I think if anyone can do it, it's you. Don't give up on her. She's gonna take some work, but if she didn't feel anything for you, we wouldn't even be discussing this right now. You would've been dropped like a bad habit; believe me," Max informs me.

Thank God for her. She's the only one that knows the true Kinsey in and out. I feel good that I have her rooting for us and on my side. "Has she spoken to you about me?" I know this is a long shot, but I just have to ask.

"She talks to me about *everything*," she says with that warning in her voice. "But, yes. We have spoken about you. And that's all I'm gonna say," she tells me with a wink. She gets up to head out.

"Aww, come on, Max!" I call after her. She motions that her lips are zipped and heads off. I lean back in my chair, running my hands through my hair. Damn! What I do know for sure is that Max told me not to give up, which means something big in my book.

The rest of the day is pretty uneventful. I had a business meeting with two of my clients and one video chat. It's now five-thirty, and Jeff is hounding me to leave already. I stop by the gas station to grab a six-pack and head over to my brother's.

This will be the first time I am entering his house on good terms. I'm actually looking forward to spending some guy time with him. I just have to keep reminding myself to let go of the past, and today begins a new chapter for us. I don't think either one of us actually mentioned our reconciliation to our parents. It's probably better this way anyways. I would hate to disappoint my mom if things head south.

Kyle answers the door with Penelope in hand. Her smile is from ear to ear when she sees me, and her arms reach out for me. This absolutely melts my heart. A quick flash of Kinsey swollen with my child takes over me as I take Penelope in my arms. I shake the thought, but it feels so right: her pregnant with my baby. Damn. I'm totally getting a little ahead of myself here.

"Who's my favorite little girl?" I say to Penelope as I tickle her. She squeals with laugher and excitement. Kyle grabs the six-pack from me, and we head into the kitchen. Penelope's new thing is to press her lips together and blow, causing spit to fly everywhere. Then she laughs. I am now covered in baby spit, but I wouldn't have it any other way.

"I see you found out her new thing," Jeff says, pointing out my now-drenched shirt.

Penelope squeals again, now smacking me in the head. I hold her hand down before she whales on me again.

"Yeah, she's learning that hitting is fun," Kyle tells me as he cracks me open a nice, cold beer. I set Penelope down in her high chair and give her some Cheerios to snack on.

"So, where did the girls head off to?" I ask before taking a nice swig of my beer.

Kyle gives Penelope her sippy cup with water. "They headed over to Tony D's. I'm kind of jealous. I could go for one of those arancini balls! Those things are amazing!" Kyle finishes, now making me hungry.

"Speaking of food, what's for dinner?" I ask.

Jeff jumps in. "Yeah, bro. I'm starving! Whatcha gonna cook for us, Mr. Chef Boyardee?" I laugh.

"What do you want me to whip up? I can defrost some sauce and make some chicken parm real quick—" Kyle suggests.

"Oh my God, yes! That shit is da bomb!" Jeff says.

I just shake my head. Where the hell did this kid learn his English? "Is that Mom's sauce recipe?" I ask Kyle.

"Hers with a twist. I think after all these years, I have finally mastered it. I heard Kinsey can cook her ass off."

I take another sip of my beer, then Penelope throws her sippy cup on the floor and laughs. I reach down and put it back on her tray. The little devil smiles as though she wants to do it again.

"Yeah, she cooks a mean greens and beans, but she's always got something in the works. I just wish I would have swallowed my pride and sat down to eat her food a long time ago," I admit to them.

Jeff gives Penelope some more Cheerios. "Yeah, bro, you're stubborn as fuck! Think of all the nights we told you to bang her and you refused!" Jeff reminds me.

"Yeah, we did say that a lot. What made you change your mind?" Kyle asks me.

I grab the chip bag from off the counter. "I don't know. Honestly, I think it was a night I came home after drinking with you guys. I was pretty buzzed, and she begged me to sit down and have a drink with her. I refused, then she said she needed me to look over some work papers with her. You know me and work; I just couldn't resist. After that night, I was a goner."

"You've fallen for her, haven't you?" Kyle asks.

I take a deep breath, because this is going to be a big one for me. "Yes. Yes, I've fallen for her." There, I finally freaking said it. I am falling in love with Kinsey. "She's all I can think about. She's the last thing I see in my mind before my eyes close at night. She's like a drug; I can't go without her, and when I do, it's almost unbearable. I want to breathe the air she breathes. I can't picture the rest of my life without her. I just don't know how to get her to see this. You guys must think I'm crazy, right?"

Jeff jumps the gun first. "No, bro! Not at all. These

are the same things we felt as well. Elise was everything to me. I didn't want to live another day without her. When you find that one person you're meant to be with, you'll know, and that shit knocks you off your ass, believe me!"

"He's right, Junior. Max took some convincing, but I just knew from the first moment I laid eyes on her that she was something special. From that moment on, I couldn't get her out of my head. It was crazy! I almost felt as though something was taking over my body," Kyle tells us, laughing. "Because, well, you know me—that just didn't happen to me."

Jeff chuckles after chugging down his beer. "Yeah, you and me both!" he adds.

I feel a little better. I know now that I'm not crazy, that's for sure. "Thanks, guys. You don't know how good it feels to hear this. I'm leaving with her in two days, and I'm going to make it my mission to break her walls down. This girl is broken, and I intend to be the one to fix her."

Penelope decides we've had enough male bonding time. She screeches for attention. "Is my little beautiful girl hungry?" Kyle asks her in baby talk. I have to say, it's cute and weird at the same time. Her smile just eats me up, though.

The rest of the night goes by smoothly with Kyle and me. He was able to put Penelope down a little early, and us guys got a quick card game in before the girls came strolling in. I could tell they had a little too much to drink, because Kinsey gets that glazed-over twinkle in her eyes. This means she's in rare form, and I need to get her home and take advantage of this.

We say our goodbyes—thankfully she left her car at home—and we head off. I turn the music to a low thrum and wait for Kins to speak. She's looking out her window, thinking at the moment. I can see her reflection through the glass, and she always gets the little crease in between her brows when she's contemplating something.

She finally looks over to me. "Junior, I like you. I really do. You're different than what I've dated in the past. I know that. I'm just asking you to please be patient with me; I need some time. I mean, we already live together, and now we're sexual together, so I need to go slow with the rest. Do you understand what I'm saying?" she asks.

They say when you drink, your true feelings come out. I don't believe she would have admitted any of this otherwise, but I'm thankful for it. It means me putting in the work isn't a waste of time.

"Yes, I completcly understand what you're saying, but I also want to add this—it's okay to be scared, because honestly, I'm scared shitless. This is all new to me too, but you're worth it to me. You're worth the risk of being hurt. Kins, I'm your friend before anything. We're kind of both jumping into this territory blind. But if you don't take that leap of faith, you'll never know what beautiful things could come from this. The only thing I'm asking from you in this moment is to just stay long enough to see the possibilities. Don't run from your feelings because you're scared. We can take this leap together."

She remains quiet after this. I pull into the parking garage, and we head up in the elevator. The air is thick and tense with the unknown, mixed with some electricity. Normally I would pounce on her, but since she has a lot on her mind, I'm going to let her make the next move.

We get off the elevator, and she turns to me.

"Okay," she says.

Hmm, what am I missing? What part is she exactly okay with? "'Okay' what, Kins?"

"Okay, I will stay long enough to see the possibilities. I can't promise anything, but I will try my best to let you in. You're a good guy, Junior, and I know you would never hurt me on purpose," she finishes.

I can't help but grab her waist and bring her into me. I need to feel those lips ASAP. I tangle my hands in her hair and touch my lips to hers. It's gentle but efficient; a voltage shoots straight down to my groan. I can't help but groan, but she slowly backs away and I sulk.

"Come on, let's get out of this hallway," she says, dragging me to our apartment door. I look around and realize I completely lost track of where we were.

As soon as I shut the door, I grab her again to bring her to me. "I've been dying to touch you all night," I whisper to her.

She drops her jacket on the floor, and I quickly unbutton her shirt. We're like two crazed teenagers that can't get enough of each other. She's driving me absolutely insane.

I drop my jacket, and she removes my shirt. I reach down, grab under her thighs, and lift her up so she is now straddling her legs around me while I walk us into my bedroom.

"Fuck me," she begs in a seductive little voice. Damn, what this woman does to me.

I rip off her pants and her tiny boy shorts that I fucking love. I unzip my pants, allowing everything to fall to the ground. I crawl over her and hold my cock at her entrance and wait until she begs for me again before I slam right into her, hard and deep.

She screams with pleasure, and I know I am hitting her perfect spot. I lift her legs over my shoulders, and I can feel the walls of her pussy tightening around me. "I'm about to come. Come for me," I demand through my teeth. I'm doing everything I can not to not bust before she does, but the more I pump into her, the more she quivers around me.

I feel her wetness pouring over me, and I let go. I lie over her, breathless, trying not to smush her as we both try to catch our breaths. What is this girl doing to me?

I kiss her forehead, each side of her cheek, and the top of her nose. The feelings that are swarming through me are strong and real. I'm overwhelmed with emotions right now.

"Damn, that was some good hardcore fucking," she says while laughing.

I look down at her with a smirk. "Oh yeah? Don't lie."

She smacks me on the arm. "Listen, stud. I don't lie. You just fucked the shit out of me, and now I'm ready for bed."

I pull out of her, and we both wince from the sensitivity. "I'm going to get us something to clean up with."

"Wait, I'm right behind you."

We clean up and crawl under my covers. I don't even have to pull her to me; she slides to my side and nooks right up to me. I turn off the bedside lamp. I'm grinning ear to ear, because she is now voluntarily sleeping beside me. Just a week ago, I had to persuade her. Thank

God it's dark so she can't see me. I close my eyes with content. Everything I've ever needed is now right beside me.

CHAPTER SEVENTEEN

Kinsey

The last two days dragged on, but it's now finally Saturday! Junior and I are packing up his car for our week in South Carolina with my parents. He doesn't seem nervous one bit. Most guys would be freaking out about meeting a girl's parents, let alone staying with them for a week. But not Junior.

He shoves in the last bag and slams the trunk closed. "Are you ready?" he asks.

I smile. This is just crazy that we're road tripping together. "I am, sexy pants!" He shakes his head at my nickname for him. I give him a wink and hop in the car.

He jumps in. "Okay, and we're off!"

I take control of the music situation before he does. I've known him for all this time, and I've never even asked what type of music he is into. I change the station to Kiss 107 pop hits, and Mike Posner is on. I see Junior's head bobbing to the music.

I laugh. I like when he loosens up; it's cute. "Is this the kind of music you like?" I ask him.

"Yeah, I like a little bit of everything. Mike Posner is actually one of my favorite artists."

"Huh, I would have tagged you as more of a classical guy. Something more serious and smart," I joke.

"Oh yeah? Interesting. I would have tagged you as more of the Brittany Spears type," he teases back.

I give him the evil eye. "You're a dick," I tell him, turning up the music.

It's been a good eight hours. We've made two pit stops, food and bathroom breaks, and now we're in need of some gas. The ride down has been nice and relaxing so far. Junior drove the first couple hours, and I drove the last.

"Did you need anything from inside?" Junior asks before getting out of the car.

"No, I'm fine. I'm just going to get out and stretch."

I step out of the car and reach my hands over my head while arching my back. My lower back cracks. I notice this gas station is a little run-down. The gas pumps are old and dented. Behind the station seems to be a junkyard of some type, full of old, run-down cars and trucks. I'm reminded of an old horror movie. This place gives me the creeps. I don't know if it's the remote area or the old man sitting outside the store smoking a cigar with no teeth. A chill runs through me.

Junior comes out of the store and heads to our pump. I quickly walk over to him, watching my surroundings. I'm sure as hell not going to be some chick that gets knocked out from behind.

"Do you fucking see this place? Hurry up, let's get out of here. This place creeps me the hell out!" I tell him.

He chuckles. "You should see the set-up inside. I wouldn't even buy a wrapped candy bar from this place. They're probably years old."

I haven't seen another car pass by yet. "Okay, awesome. Now can you please hurry up before we end up as fresh meat for the cannibals?"

Junior snickers and shakes his head. "Just get into the car, woman. I'm almost done."

We finally pull off, and I immediately let out a deep breath of air. I feel safe again. "Are you good now?" he asks me, smirking.

"Yes. Why do you find this so funny? Haven't you ever seen *Texas Chainsaw Massacre*?" I ask.

"It's just that I've never seen you so nervous, Miss. I'm not scared of anything," he teases.

"Well, I'm scared about getting eaten alive, and I'm scared of many other things that are out of my control. Not getting killed happens to be in my control at the moment," I advise him. I turn to him. "What's the last thing you were scared of?"

He rubs his chin, which now has some scruff showing. I have to admit; he looks mighty sexy with that rough scruff. He looks a little edgy and dangerous. My sexy man. Shit. Did I really just think that?

"Hmm, the last time I felt scared, huh? It was when you texted me to come get you from Jax's place. I thought he may have put his hands on you. I was ready to go in there and kill the son of a bitch! That's the moment I realized you are more than just a friend to me, Kins."

Damn, I didn't mean for this to get so deep. "Yeah, that was a pretty awkward moment, but if he would have put his hands on me, he would have been dead before you got there, believe me. I would have beat his ass even worse."

Junior laughs. Good, I needed the mood lightened up a bit. "So, tell me, what was Max like when you first met her?"

I pull out my Chapstick and apply some to my dry lips. "Whoa! She was a hot mess. Can we say tomboy? She had on some old Jordache jeans and an oversized T-shirt with stains. Her hair was thrown in a messy bun, and I don't think she had used makeup nor knew what it was. It took some work, but I finally turned her around. She's stubborn and fought me every step of the way, especially when it came to wearing heels, but I won. I always do! And look at her now—you would never know," I tell him, pretty proud of myself.

Junior looks a little shocked. "Wow, that's crazy. Jeff told me a little bit about her life growing up. Her parents were real assholes to her and her brothers. I hated hearing about all of it; it made me sick," he says.

I look out my window at the forest. Birds fly from the trees into the blue, free sky. So symbolic of what we're discussing now. "Yes, they were horrible. Her brother, Luke, got the brunt of it. Even though him and I don't really see eye to eye, I still have complete respect for the man he is, because of that. He endured all that pain so Max and her younger brother, Justin, didn't have to. Max is a strong chick, but what I love now is that she doesn't have to be, because Kyle can be strong for her."

Junior snorts. I quickly look over at him, ready to be combative. "You know; I can say the same about you. You're a mighty strong woman, but you don't always have to be. I could be strong for you if you'd let me," he offers. He doesn't say another word. He waits for me to speak. I'm feeling as though seconds are turning into minutes, and minutes are turning into hours before I'm able to speak again.

"Junior, we're just friends who have sex. That's all. Now can you please stop with all this mushy bullshit before I put some earplugs in for the rest of the ride?" I threaten him. He just shakes his head.

"You just told me to be patient with you, and now this? You're impossible, Kins," he says under his breath.

I pretend not to hear and jack the volume up on the music. For the rest of the ride, we can just be.

I finally see the big green sign that says Myrtle Beach, South Carolina. I start jumping up and down in my seat. I am so excited to see my parents. It's late Saturday evening. I text my mom quickly to let her know we'll be there shortly.

Junior laughs at my enthusiasm. "You're excited to be home, huh?"

My smile is from ear to ear. "Yes, very much so. It feels as though I haven't been here in forever! Are you ready to meet the parents?" I ask.

He shrugs his shoulders. "Yeah, sure. What's the big deal? We're just friends, so no pressure, right?"

I guess I didn't think of it like that. "Right."

The GPS takes us right to the house. My parents

live in a little cottage right off the beach. They bought it when we moved. It was perfect for me; it was like my own little sanctuary. I needed the peace and serenity after everything that happened in high school. I used to sit out on the beach alone and stare at the stars to clear my mind from all the fog.

"This is a cool place. You didn't tell me they lived right on the beach," Junior says.

"Once we get settled in, I'll take you out to my favorite spot."

We pull into the driveway. "Sounds good. Oh, I think your parents are coming out," he tells me, looking toward the front door. Of course they are. They are dying to meet this new man in my life. There's no way my mother is going to accept the "just friends" routine. She'll take one look at us and know there's more to it than I'm allowing myself to admit. If only I could just separate my feelings from sex, but who am I kidding? It's not just the sex I enjoy; it's the whole stinking package.

I jump out of the car and rush into my mom's arms. "Hi, Mama. I've missed you."

She squeezes me a little tighter as she begins to sniffle. "I've missed you too, dear. It's so quiet around here without you popping up," she tells me. I always showed up for dinner after work. It sure beat having to cook for myself.

We let go, and she looks over at Junior. I give my daddy a big squeeze, and he kisses me on top of my head like he has since I was a little girl.

"Well, welcome to South Carolina, Junior. My, my, you're a handsome thing," my mother says while giving him a hug and a kiss on the cheek.

"It's nice to meet you, Mrs. Balterson. Your home looks beautiful. Thank you for having me," Junior complements, and she melts like butter. I roll my eyes at him and he smirks.

"Please, call me Kat. It's short for Katherine, and this is George—"

He walks toward my dad with his hand out. My father shakes his hand nice and strong. "It's nice to meet you, Junior. Our home is your home. Here, let me help you with the bag." My father follows Junior to the back of car. I grab my small bag from the backseat and walk into the house with my mom.

I stop as soon as I get in the door and take a whiff. The house smells of the beach. I look around before heading upstairs; everything looks the same. My mom decorated the house years ago just like a beach house/ vacation home: blues and whites with seashells all over, including the wall art.

"Go get settled in, dear. I'll show Junior his room. Would you like me to put a pot of coffee on, or do you want some wine?" she asks.

Ugh. I could totally go for both. "Um, I could go for some wine."

I head upstairs with my bag. My room isn't huge. Big enough for a double bed, dresser, desk, and a small walk-in closet. The best part is the little window sill I used to sit on while looking out to the ocean. At night, I could hear the waves crashing against the shore before falling asleep. I used to just lie in my bed and fall asleep to it.

I hear my father helping Junior up the stairs with our suitcases. They set up the extra bedroom across the hallway for him. It was either that or the den downstairs. I think they know exactly what they're up to.

I sit on my bed and lay back, sprawling my legs and arms out. After being in the car for over twelve hours, this feels amazing. I hear the floor of my room creak. I look up and Junior is leaning against the door frame, watching me.

"Hey," I say.

He strolls over to me and kneels down on the bed in between my legs. We both gaze at each other without a word said. It's intense and full of promise. God, I want him. I want him inside of me so damn bad—and then I remember where we are.

I quickly sit up before he locks me down with his hands and body. "Junior, my parents are right downstairs," I whisper. He chuckles. He backs up and helps me off the bed. "Come, let's go downstairs. They have some wine waiting for us." I grab his hand to lead him downstairs. I let go as soon as we reach the bottom of the stairs—don't want any misconceptions.

"Did you two get settled in?" my mom asks.

"Yes, we did," Junior replies. We sit down at the kitchen table with my father, and Mom hands us our glasses of wine.

"So how was the trip in?" Mom asks.

I take a sip of the pinot noir. This is my mother's and my favorite. "Long! Next time I'm flying. Screw the drive!"

My father laughs. "Well, I'm glad you had Junior here to keep you company. I would have been worried if you drove here by yourself," my father says.

My mother finishes putting the cream and sugar in her coffee. "How's Maxine? I haven't seen her in ages! How's that beautiful baby of hers?"

"She's good, Mama, and that little Penelope is amazing! She's already getting so big. You should see it; she has Junior here wrapped around her little finger," I tell them, laughing. Penelope at less than a year old already knows what she's doing. The boys better watch out when she gets older!

"Yes, she does. It's crazy how such a little girl can be so demanding already. My brother is in for it when she gets older," Junior informs them.

My dad jumps in. "I wouldn't doubt it. This one here gave us a run for our money. She was always untamable, even as a little girl!"

Junior chuckles while taking all this information in. "Okay, okay, please refrain from bringing out the naked pictures. I know that's coming next," I tell them.

We all chat for another hour or so, and a couple glasses of wine. "Well, you two must be exhausted. I know I am. I have to go to the shop early tomorrow. It's shipment day. Kins, will you be coming with me?" my mom asks.

"I think I'm gonna sleep in and hang out here for the day—maybe show Junior around some."

My father says goodnight and heads to their room. They don't have to go far; their master suite is set up on the first floor. "Okay, sounds good, dear. I'll set the coffee pot for ten o'clock tomorrow." She comes over to kiss me on the cheek goodnight. Somehow this always makes me feel like a little girl. She hated when I got too old to tuck in bed. I think she sat outside my room crying, because I was ready to be big.

We are now alone. I refill our wineglasses and grab my sweater from the back of my chair. "Come on. I want to show you the night's sky out here," I tell Junior, giving him his full wineglass back.

I open the sliding glass door that leads to the back deck. It's extremely chilly. The moon is shining brightly as the waves crash to the shore. I take my shoes off, and Junior does the same, then we head out onto the sand. We walk up to the water. "Look," I tell him, pointing up to the sky. The stars blanket the dark night like glistening diamonds. They're every which way you look. This end of the beach doesn't have a lot of houses, so it stays dark, making the stars so much easier to see.

Junior looks up. "Wow, this is unbelievable!" he comments, looking up.

"Come," I take his hand and lead him over to the rocks. There's one particular rock that is tucked nicely away by the other rocks, almost like a small cave without a top. It has always been my perfect hideaway. It's still open enough to see the water and the stars but closed enough so no one can see you.

Junior follows me as I climb the rocks. It's a little tough only using one hand and not trying to spill my wine in the other. "Be careful," he warns me.

We get to the rock, and I take a seat on the edge, allowing my legs to swing over the side. I pat the space next to me, and Junior takes the seat. "So, this is your little spot, huh?" he asks.

"Yup, this is my thinking spot. I spent many nights out here," I inform him. Even though it's dark, the moon gives just enough light for me to see. Junior studies me intently.

"How many guys have you brought out here?" he questions.

I look over to him. "None. You're the first."

His brows furrow. "Don't lie," he says.

Maybe it's time I told him about my past, then he might understand me a bit more. After Tommy, I didn't start dating again until I was in college. Even back then, I rarely went on second or third dates. I take a deep breath, and I dive in.

He listens intently without interrupting, only

asking a couple of questions here and there. Afterwards, we sit quietly, gazing at the stars. The wind blows lightly, loosening the little hairs in front of my face. Junior moves them and tucks them behind my ears. "Kins, I want you to know I would never let anything bad happen to you. I want to be by your side so I can protect you, even if it's just being your friend. Thank you for finally letting me in. You have amazing parents for taking you away from the hurt and bringing you here."

A little tear drops from my eye. I don't know what is coming over me, but I have to touch him. I need him to wrap his arms around me tight. I turn to him and climb over his legs to straddle him. I don't want to waste another minute. I smash my lips against his. His fingers dig into my back as he brings me closer to him.

"God, Kins, you are so damn beautiful," he whispers to me as the waves crash the shore behind me.

I slip my hands under his shirt, feeling his sexy ripples as I go. "Just kiss me, please?" I beg in a sexy, sweet voice. He does exactly what I ask, and boy, does he freaking kiss me! All his need for me, passion, and hotness are wrapped into this one kiss. His tongue delves into my mouth, leading me through the sexy tango with him. He's so damn good with his tongue. I get wet just thinking about this. The things this man can do with that tongue should be illegal. He knows exactly what he is doing.

He then makes his way down my jaw to the nape of my neck and nibbles softly on my earlobe. I moan with pleasure as I grind over his hard cock. He feels as though he's going to bust right through the seams of his jeans.

I grab the hem of his T-shirt and lift it over his head. His chiseled body belongs in an art museum. He slips my hoodie off and lifts my shirt over my head. I shiver from the breeze, but I'm anything but cold. I reach behind me and unsnap my bra, allowing it to fall down my arms.

Junior kisses down my neck, over my collarbone, and grabs my breast. He takes my hard, erect nipple between his teeth. I immediately arch my back and moan. He nips and sucks as he tugs my other nipple between his fingers. I continue to grind over him and he groans.

His groan spreads fire through my body, licking every inch of me, landing right between my thighs. If I don't feel him inside of me real soon, I'm going to explode. I begin to unbutton his pants, and he unbuttons mine. I remove each pant leg and underwear. I hold myself right above the head of his cock. Neither of us move, except for our heaving chests.

The stars, the waves, the wind all make this moment so much more. Feelings swarm through me like I've never felt before. I put my hands on the sides of his face and rub my thumbs down his cheeks. He's so perfect. I've never seen him—I mean, *really* seen him until now.

I slowly push down on him, our eyes still locked, and he takes my hips and pushes me down the rest of the way. "*Shit!* You feel so good," Junior grunts out through his clamped teeth. I kiss him and begin moving over him, slow and precise. Each and every time I move forward, the tip of his dick hits my special spot.

I feel my insides beginning to overheat as the tide of pleasure creeps up over me. His fingernails dig into my hips the closer he gets to release. "Come for me, Kins! I'm gonna come any minute, and I want you to come with me," he says, trying to hold off. I grind over him one last time, and we both explode like fireworks. Every last bit of energy has been drained. I wrap my arms around him and lean my head against his chest. His heart sounds like thunder against my ear. He runs his finger up and down my spine as we sit like this for a long while.

"Kins, don't you see—we're perfect together." I don't respond, because I don't want to say the wrong thing. I don't want to lead him on. The wind blows hard, and I shiver. "Come on, let's get back to the house," Junior instructs.

We quickly get dressed, sneak into the house quietly as though we are two teenagers about to get caught, and tiptoe up the stairs. We stop in the hallway outside our rooms. I almost want to ask him to stay with me, but I think it's more appropriate to sleep apart under my parents' roof. I kiss him goodnight and shut the door behind me. I flop down on my bed, close my eyes, and listen to the waves as I fall asleep.

CHAPTER EIGHTEEN

Junior

I wake up to the smell of fresh coffee and the feel of a soft beach breeze flowing through my window. Last night was almost perfect. Kinsey opened up to me about her past, allowing me to understand the reason behind her madness. I could also see a small change in her that I know she felt. We connected in a way that we never have before. I don't know if it was the surroundings and being under the magical stars or if it was her letting some of her guard down, but it just felt so right.

I throw a pair of jeans and a T-shirt on and head downstairs. Kinsey is already sitting at the table, drinking coffee with her father. "Good morning," I say to the both of them.

"Good morning, Junior. How did you sleep last night?" George asks.

I pour my coffee into the mug they left out. "I slept amazingly well," I tell him, winking at Kins. She just rolls her eyes and takes a sip of her coffee. It's true though, I knocked out as soon as my head hit the pillow.

"Good to hear. What are you two up to today?" he asks.

"Well, I figured I would take him to breakfast over at Ma's Diner. They make the best omelets!" she answers. "And then show him around town a bit. Maybe you guys can go to the marina tomorrow so I can head to the shop with Mom for a while?" Kins suggests.

"Yeah, that's not a bad idea. That'll give Junior and I some time to get to know each other. I mean, you two are living together and everything, so it only seems appropriate," her father agrees.

I stay standing against the kitchen counter. "Sounds good to me. You work with Maxine's brother, right?" I ask George.

He finishes up his coffee and gets up to put his cup in the sink. Kinsey looks more like her father than she does her mother, though she got lucky by inheriting her mother's blue eyes. Her father still has a lot of years on him, and he's kept in good shape. I would almost bet he still goes to the gym on the regular. His skin is tan and leathery; you can definitely tell he's spent a lot of years in the sun.

"Yes, Luke. He's a great guy. He's actually going up to New York in another month or so to visit with Maxine and the baby. You'll be able to meet him tomorrow," he tells me. He claps his hands together and looks to Kins and I. "Okay, I'm heading into work for a bit. Call me if you need anything, and you two have fun today. I know how hard my little girl works, so take it easy, will ya?" he advises Kinsey and I.

I nod. "Yes, sir. I'll make sure she relaxes today."

"Oh geeze," Kinsey gripes. "Yes, Daddy. I'll take it easy. Have a good day at work," she yells to him as he walks out the front door.

I chuckle, and she looks over at me. "What?" she questions.

"Daddy, huh? You can call me 'Daddy' if you'd like to," I tease.

She throws a napkin at me. "You're such a freaking ass!" she says. I can tell she's trying to be serious, but she just can't help smiling. "Are you ready to go?"

"Yeah, I'm starving! You took all my energy last night. I need to replenish so I'm ready for tonight."

I follow her out the door. "Who says you're getting any tonight?"

I run up behind her and tickle her sides. She laughs and tries to squirm away. I love the sound of her laugh. She sounds so happy and carefree; I love that it's me making her sound this way.

"Okay, okay! Maybe I'll be nice tonight. *But* only if you stop tickling me!" she says in between laughs. I immediately stop and head to the car. "I'm going to get you for that, you know!"

We head over to the breakfast place. I order one of the special omelets and french toast; she orders the same. I know why they call this restaurant Ma's Diner. It's cozy, small, and it feels like Mom's literally cooking in the kitchen. Some of the people look like regulars, almost like they could be a fixture in the restaurant.

There's a group of teenage kids at the back table ogling Kinsey. I really want to tell them to screw off, but it's not worth it. They're just a bunch of hormone-crazed boys just like Kyle was at that age.

    The waitress comes to deliver our food and refill our coffees. "Holy crap! These omelets are freaking *huge*!" I say in shock.

    Kinsey laughs. "I told you! These are their specialty. So they just added a new bookstore in town. You wanna go check it out with me? We need to see what is up-and-coming. You know it's always good to look at the competition. Plus, I need a book to dig into while we lounge on the back deck this week."

    "Max told me that you want to start writing, is that true?" I ask her.

    She swallows her bite of food. "She told you? Yeah, it was just a thought. I've always loved writing; I've just never really had the time to. I don't even know what I would write, anyways."

    "Just sit your butt in a chair, pull up a blank file, and just write. Isn't that what us agents tell our authors when they have writer's block? You have to start somewhere, and you're not on any deadline, so start out writing for an hour a day. See where that takes you," I tell her, trying my hardest to motivate her. "I'll help be your beta reader."

She laughs. "Okay, maybe you're right. I'm going to enjoy my time off, but once we get back to Rochester, I'm going to attempt it. You just have to promise not to laugh at anything you read, okay?"

I grin. This makes me extremely happy. "I would never, and I most definitely promise, Kins. I think you'll be amazing."

We finish up breakfast and head over to the new bookstore. It's like a candy store for agents. Afterwards, we spend the rest of the day roaming around town. It's beautiful out—a sunny, warm seventy degrees. It's the perfect day, because I'm spending it with the perfect girl. I grab her hand and entwine my fingers with hers as we walk down the main pier. I expected her to pull away, but to my surprise, she didn't.

We sit down on the bench at the end of the pier looking over the water. It's not busy, but it's not private either. Families walk together hand-in-hand, and it reminds me of what I want for myself—what I want with Kinsey.

I peek over at her as she stares out to the water. The breeze flows through her hair, the sun shines on her beautiful, fair skin, and as I look at her—I mean, *really* look at her—I realize that I have completely fallen in love with this woman. She is 100 percent it for me. I love every part of her crazy, neurotic ass. I just wish I could tell her.

"Hey there, what's going on in that mind of yours?" I ask her.

She looks over at me and smiles. "I'm just thinking that I'm glad you're here with me." There's no need for her to say anything else. Just that short sentence made my day. I smile big and bring her hand up to my lips to kiss it.

We stay here for a little bit longer, enjoying each other's company in silence, and then head back to her parent's house for dinner.

"Well hello, you two! How was your day?" Kat asks.

"It was good, Mama. Where's Daddy?"

Her mom is setting the plates of food in the middle of the table. I walk over and start helping. "Thank you, dear."

"Your dad is just getting out of the shower. He'll be in in a minute. Come have a seat. Do you both want some wine?"

"No, not tonight. Do you have any beer? I should have asked you before we got here. I could have stopped at the store," Kinsey says. A beer sounds nice right about now.

Kat puts the last dish down on the table. "Actually, your father brought some Coronas home. I have some lime in the refrigerator, also."

"I'll grab them." I take out the lime and beer, making my way around the kitchen for the knives and a cutting board. I bring Kinsey hers. Her father comes out from his bedroom, and I hold up a beer to him. He nods.

I bring him his beer. He thanks me. "Wow, this spread looks amazing, Kat!" I take my seat next to Kinsey and give her a quick wink.

"Thank you, Junior." I wait for someone else to make the first move. I'm not quite sure what their traditions may be, so I'm going to follow suit.

Kinsey loads her plate first and then passes the

plates of food around. "How was it down at the marina today, George?" I inquire.

I take a bite of chicken, and it's amazing. Kinsey must notice my pleasured face, because she chuckles quietly to herself.

"Busy. Everyone's beginning to load their boats into storage. The weather begins to get cold like this and people get forced to wheel them in. We have a shop, too, that does tune-ups and any other work that needs to be done before they store them away," he explains.

Kinsey finishes taking a sip of her beer. "What time will you be going down there tomorrow?" she asks him.

"I was thinking I would sleep in a bit in the morning. I mean, after all, Junior is here on vacation. How does eleven sound?" George asks me.

I nod and swallow my chicken. "Sounds perfect."

"I'll make my special pancakes tomorrow before you two head off," Kat offers.

"Yum!" Kinsey adds. "Her pancakes are the best! I had to tell her to stop making them, because I was gaining ten pounds each time I came over here!"

I chuckle. I highly doubt that. I feel her foot against mine. She then begins to trail her foot up my shin. I freeze. Is this really happening right now? The last thing I need to be doing is speaking to her parents with a boner. I clear my throat and move my leg over an inch.

She looks at me with the grin of a devil. I am so going to get her for this! I push my chair back. "Would anyone like another beer?"

"Yes, please," George says.

"You know what? I'll take one too," Kat says.

I nod and head to the refrigerator. "Coming right up!" I look over at Kinsey, and she puts on a little pouty face. I want to run over there and bite that damn lip.

"Mama, do you have a lot of inventory to do tomorrow? You just had a big shipment come in, right?"

I hand them both their beers, and they thank me. "I did most of it today. It wasn't a huge shipment this weekend, but I could use some help stocking," her mother informs her.

I bring Kinsey her beer and make sure to put a little

distance between us this time. It's funny, her parents seem so kind and laidback. Where the hell did she get her spitfire personality from?

"Oh, Geena came to see me at the store. I told her you were in town and invited her over for dinner tomorrow night. I hope you don't mind?" she asks Kinsey. She then looks to me. "Geena is Kinsey's cousin. They were pretty close growing up," Kat explains to me.

"No, that's fine with me. I haven't seen her in forever! What's she been up to?"

Kat takes a nice swig of her beer. She's such a tiny lady; it looks as though the beer bottle might swallow her up. "Well, she just went back to school to get her bachelor's for her RN. So she works full-time at the hospital and has classes in her free time. Poor thing, I don't think she has much of a personal life. My sister said she hasn't had time for any dating. You girls and your careers! When are you ever going to make time to start a family?"

Oh boy, that was a loaded question. Kinsey looks a little offended. "Mama, it's not every girl's dream to get married and start a family. This isn't the fifties any longer. I have dreams and goals that I want to fulfill before any of that."

"Oh, Kins. You've been career-oriented for years now. It's not going anywhere. There's no reason you can't have both. I mean, look at Maxine for Christ's sake." Kat then looks at me. "What are your hopes for the future?" she questions.

Wow. How the hell did this turn onto me? "I hope to have a family one day. There's no reason you can't have both a family and career these days as long as you have two hands-on parties to make it easier. I think once Kinsey finds Mr. Right, she'll feel differently," I reply.

Kinsey rolls her eyes. "Oh give me a break! You're such a girl! You and your damn soul mate crap," she tells me, basically ripping me a new asshole in front of her parents.

"*Kinsey!*" her mom scolds. "Junior here just knows what he wants. There's nothing wrong with that! Don't mind her; she's always been a firecracker. I don't know where she gets it from."

George just laughs, completely entertained by all

of this. After this conversation, we keep the rest of the dinner light. I help Kat clean up while Kinsey sits in the living room with her father. Her mother grabs my wrist and faces me. "I just want you to know that my Kinsey has on a hard-armored exterior, but on the inside, she's loving and vulnerable. She's just afraid. She needs the right man to let her guard down, and I believe that man is you."

I'm a little caught off guard. I wasn't expecting this. "Thank you for believing in me. Your daughter is extremely special to me," I admit.

Kat's eyes tear up. "Bless you, dear. This news brings me so much joy. I can feel it in my heart that you are the one for her, even if she doesn't know it yet. Though, I've seen the way she looks at you when you are not paying any attention, and I know she feels the same way. I talk to Maxine every now and then, and she's told me what an amazing man you are. I just hope Kinsey stops being stubborn enough to see what she has in front of her," she finishes.

"What are you two up to in here?" Kinsey questions, looking back and forth between us.

Kat puts away the last clean dish out of the dishwasher. "Nothing, dear. I'm just trying to get to know your friend here. I think Dad and I are going to turn in for the night," she advises. She gives me a squeeze on the shoulder and kisses Kinsey good night.

"Night, Mama."

It's just Kinsey and I, alone.

"So, what were you guys really talking about? I know when my mom is lying," Kinsey interrogates.

I chuckle. She is just too much sometimes. "Your mom is a sweet lady. I think my mother and her would get along well. Do you want another beer?"

"Yes. Let's drink it on the back deck," she suggests.

I follow her out and sit in the chair beside her. The stars are twinkling in the night's sky. There are only a couple of clouds floating and the moon is shining brightly tonight.

"I think I could definitely live out here. I'm sick of the cold weather and am not looking forward to the snow in Rochester. Out here, it is just calming and relaxing. Have you ever thought about moving back?" I ask her.

She thinks for a moment after swigging down some beer. "I have actually. I'm not so sure New York is the place for me in the long run. I figure I'll give it another year or two and maybe head back this way. I have no idea what I would do without Max, though."

"Max will do just fine on her own. She has Kyle. Besides, if you start writing, you can do that career anywhere. My parents have always talked about Kyle and I taking over their part of the agency, but I think Kyle and Max can handle it on their own. I was thinking maybe I could open up my own agency. Just handle a couple of clients and cut back on my workload. I've saved more than enough money over the years to do just that and live comfortably," I explain to her.

"Junior, can I ask you something?"

"Sure."

"What happens to me once you find a woman you like? You know it's bound to happen. We can't be roommates forever."

"I've already found her, and I'm hoping to be your roommate for the rest of our lives," I admit. This may scare her away, but I'm willing to take that chance. She needs to know how I feel.

"Junior—" she says softly. Here it comes. She's going to push me away.

I stop her. "I know, we're just friends. That may be how you feel, but it's not the way I feel. It started out that way for me, but you're becoming much more. Kins, I lo—"

She quickly stands up. "Don't you dare, Junior! Don't you dare ruin what we have!" she yells, not letting me finish or say another word. She opens the sliding glass door and storms inside, leaving me in the dust. Well, that went well.

I stay out here for a bit longer and then head upstairs to my room. I stop at her door for a moment, but I decide to keep moving. Now is not the time to hash this out. It's been a long day, and I think we could both use a good night's sleep. I won't give up, no matter how hard she kicks and screams.

I open my window and then lay down on my bed with my arms folded behind my head. I hear my door creak open and see Kinsey walking in and closing the door behind her. I don't say a word as she climbs up my bed and begins to kiss me. I allow her to take the lead, letting her undress me.

Tonight there's no speaking. It's just her and I and the waves crashing against the shore. We don't fuck, we make love, and it's the most passionate and the most liberating moment of my life. Kinsey sets herself free, finally allowing herself to feel. She pushes down her fear while allowing me to show her love.

We fall asleep naked in each other's arms, tired and satisfied. This is what our life could be like if she would just let us happen.

"So, tell me George, how did you and Kinsey's mother meet?" I ask him as we head to the marina.

"She and I were in high school together. She's originally from Charleston, but her parents moved to Greenville during freshman year. The first moment I laid eyes on her, I knew she was the only one for me. It took me a while to approach her. Every guy sought out to be with her, and I just didn't want to be the next Joe Schmo adding to the lineup. I had to make her notice me. I needed to stand out," he tells me.

"I finally made my move, and it was history from that moment on. We've never been apart. Sometimes it takes patience and perseverance to get the end result you want. But it was all worth it in the end. You understand what I'm saying, son?"

"Yes, I most certainly do," I reply.

We make it to the marina, and I finally get to meet Max's brother, Luke. He seems like a good guy, extremely serious but good. We spoke about my brother and about our niece, Penelope. He's sad he has missed out on so much of her first couple of months. Max doesn't have a relationship with her parents. I guess her father has been calling Luke, asking Luke to reach out to Max on his behalf so he can meet his granddaughter. Kyle would never allow that unless Max was totally onboard with it. Luke refuses to have any part of it. I don't blame him.

The rest of the day goes by fast. I played third wheel most of the day, helping out when I could. The work actually wasn't that bad. Being outside is a bonus as well, but I have to admit, I spent a lot of extra time wondering what Kinsey was doing all day and if she'd thought about me as well.

We pull up to the house, and I see an extra car in the driveway. It must be Kinsey's cousin, Geena. I go straight upstairs to jump into the shower. I'm sweaty and need to freshen up a bit. I head downstairs, feeling completely refreshed and unbelievably starving.

"Well hello, Junior! How was your day with George?" Kat asks me, immediately handing me a beer. I'm beginning to really like this woman.

"It was good. It was nice to see what the marina is all about," I tell her. I see a petite blonde with big green eyes staring at me from behind Kinsey in the kitchen. I walk over to her with my hand out. "You must be Geena, Kinsey's cousin. I've heard so much about you!"

She giggles, and her cheeks turn a light pink. "It's nice to meet you as well," she says with a twinkle in her eye. I see Kinsey eyeing us from the side.

Kinsey steps in between us. "Junior, you must be

exhausted. Why don't you go have a seat at the table? Hmm, this is odd. If I didn't know any better, I would think she is a bit jealous. I like this side of her. I know she cares whether she wants to admit it or not.

Geena comes over and takes a seat next to me. Kinsey looks irritated. "So, Geena, I heard you are going back to school for your RN?" I ask.

"I am. It's a lot of work, but the benefits outweigh the cons. I can work less hours for more money once I graduate. I'm looking to work on the maternity ward. I may have to work the crap shifts, but I'll eventually work my way up. I heard you are a literary agent. I think that line of work is really fascinating. How do you pick your authors?" she asks.

"It takes some skill and a lot of it comes from gut feelings. Sometimes you just click with a writer, and if you believe in them enough, magical things can happen. I've gotten the opportunity to discover a lot of amazing authors," I answer.

"Wow. It's like the fate of others relies solely on you. That's some pretty powerful stuff."

She turns her attention to Kinsey. "And Kins, are you still the assistant for Maxine?"

"Yup, that is I—the assistant," she responds, clearly annoyed.

I jump in. "Well, I would say she's way more than an assistant. We all sort of rely on her. She docs the behind-the-scenes work for Max, but she helps out with all of us," I add.

Geena pays no mind to what I've just said. "Do you have any children, Junior?"

"Nope. No children for me. Not yet anyways." I take a swig of my beer. Kinsey's parents take a seat at the table after bringing over the plates of grilled chicken, corn on the cob, and some cornbread. "Wow! This looks delicious! I am starving."

"I concur," George adds.

"Well dig in, you two," Kat tells us. "Geena, it's so great to see you. You need to come visit more often. How's your father?"

"He's doing okay. He's still stuck on Mom after two years of being split up. She's moved on, and I just wish he would," Geena reveals.

Kat finishes her cornbread. "Oh honey, I know. Divorce is always such a sad thing to watch. Your father will eventually move on; he just needs more time. I wouldn't stress over it. He's a grown man, and you already have enough going on in your life."

We finish up dinner, and I head out to the back deck to relax. I hear the sliding glass door open and close, and I figure it's Kinsey. A hand slides up my back as I'm standing against the deck railing. I look to my right, and it's Geena. Shit! This is awkward. I move myself over an inch as her shoulder hits mine.

I wait for her to say something. "So, Junior, are you seeing anyone?" she comes straight out and asks.

"Yes, sort of."

She narrows her eyes at me. "So, it's not serious then. I was hoping to maybe get together with you before you leave this week. I have Thursday night off, and I would love to take you out to dinner."

Holy cow, she has no fear. I hear the sliding door open again. I look behind me, and it's Kinsey. She looks back and forth between the two of us, and I make sure to give the help-me-please eyes. I think she gets the hint. She comes up to the other side of me and begins to rub my arm.

"What are the two of you talking about?" Kinsey asks as Geena eyes her hand on my arm.

"Wait, is my cousin the 'sort of' girl?" Geena asks while putting air quotations up.

I chuckle. "Yes, she may be."

Kinsey looks confused. "Your cousin asked if I was seeing anyone. I answered, 'yes, sort of,'" I explain to her.

"Kins, you should have told me," Geena says to her.

She shrugs. "It's complicated. It's not something we've been sharing with anyone really."

"Well, I'm going to go," she says, giving both of us hugs. "Kins, I would hold on to him. He's seems like a great catch."

We wait until the door closes before we speak again. "So I guess I'm a pretty great catch, huh?"

She smacks my arm. "I may throw you back if you don't shut up!"

"Well, we know who might want to pick me back up—" I tease, bumping her shoulder with mine. Kinsey rolls her eyes. "You know, someday those eyes might get stuck. Then what will you do?"

"Listen, smart ass, if you don't shut up, I'm going to sit on your face to shut you up," she warns. My dick automatically gets hard.

I grab her waist and pull her to me. "Is that a promise, Miss Balterson?"

She bites her bottom lip, trying to be modest. Too bad I know her. "Do you want to meet me upstairs?" I look in toward the house. "They turned in already," she assures me.

I take her hand and drag her upstairs.

The rest of the week was amazing. We spent the days hanging and relaxing on the beach. She showed me all her favorite spots as a teenager, and we had dinner with her parents every evening. They're kind, loving people, and I have no qualms about them being a part of my future. We spent every moment together, and now our time here comes to an end tomorrow.

I know we live together, but here there's no work, no friends, no Jax, or any other distractions. I don't feel as though I have to share her. I guess I was just getting used to having her all to myself, so I'm a little bummed we're leaving.

I get out of the shower and head into my room. I stop dead in my tracks. Here Kinsey is, on my bed—naked and looking beautiful and sexy as hell. I've just now fallen even more in love with her, if that is possible.

She reaches for me to come to her. I drop my towel right where I'm standing and walk toward her. I kneel on the bed and kiss her like I've never kissed her before. I want her to feel everything I am feeling. "You are so gorgeous, Kins. You're perfect in every way possible, and you're driving me absolutely wild," I tell her. Before she can respond, I lay her down, spread her legs apart, and just gaze at her pretty pussy. I want to memorize every single inch of her, and now I want to taste every inch of her.

I start at the inside of her thighs, kissing and

nibbling my way up. I graze my nose over her clit lightly, and she bucks up. I've barely even touched her, and she's going crazy. I hold her hips down with my left hand and begin to run my finger up and down her soaking wet slit.

I graze her clit and rotate my finger in small circles over it until I hear her moan. I have to remind her to be quiet, because we're not alone. I slowly drag my finger down, circling her dripping wet passage. I then dip two of my fingers deep inside of her, and she cries out but quickly covers her mouth. Her parents are right downstairs.

I get her nice and worked up, circling her clit with the tip of my tongue and licking my way down to her ass. I circle her perfect, puckered asshole with my tongue, and she goes crazy. I do one last swipe straight up the middle, landing on her clit. As soon as I enter my fingers deep inside of her again, her walls contract and she completely comes undone.

I just have to taste her sweet, creamy come, so I dip my tongue straight into her. She takes in quick breaths while trying to back up. "Oh my God, Junior. Shit! I'm too sensitive! *Fuck!*" she cries out. Damn she tastes so fucking good though.

If she thinks she's sensitive now, just wait until I slam my cock deep into her. I push her knees back so she is now open and wide for me. There's nothing more beautiful than this sight right here. I hold my dick at her wet, slick entrance and then push into her deep and hard. She screams out, and I have to cover her mouth for her this time.

"Shhh," I tell her while chuckling. I continue my assault on her, pumping into her over and over. I slow down and pull out, sliding my cock over her glistening, wet pussy. I love watching myself slide in and out of her. This is mine. Her pussy is *all* mine. I need to hear it from her.

"Who's pussy is this?" I ask as I slam back into her. She sucks her breath in.

"Your pussy," she moans out.

"Only mine?" I question her.

I lick my thumb and rub it over her clit. She cries out again. "Only yours!" she tells me.

This makes me one happy man. I push into her in fast, rhythmic pumps while rubbing her clit, and I can feel her convulsing around me. I can't hold back any longer. I groan loudly, not being able to control myself as I have the most intense orgasm of my life.

I fall on top of her. We lie here, breathless and panting. God, I don't want to leave this place. It's been such a magical week with her. She's finally opening up to me, and she *finally* let the reigns go so I could be in control of her. This is twice now. I think she's beginning to trust me.

I grab my towel from my floor and clean us both up. She climbs under my sheet, and we fall fast asleep, wrapped in each other's arms. This is the meaning of pure bliss.

CHAPTER NINETEEN

Kinsey

Today I have to say goodbye to my parents. This week with them was amazing, and they accepted Junior in like he was already their son. Junior and my father pack the last suitcase in the trunk.

"Well, it looks like you are all set to go!" my father says to the both of us. He looks bummed. Junior reaches his hand out for a handshake, but my father skips it and goes for a hug instead. "Take care of my baby girl," he tells Junior.

"I most definitely will, George."

Of course my mother is blubbering, so the moment I take one look at her, I start tearing up as well. "Mama, we'll be back soon. You and Daddy need to come visit too, okay?"

"Yes, we plan on it, dear. Please drive safely," she says while giving me huge hug. I say goodbye to my father, and Junior says his goodbyes to my mother. I can tell she completely adores Junior, and she asks him to come back soon.

We jump in the car and wave goodbye as we pull out of the driveway and head off. It's such a bittersweet moment. I hate leaving them, but I'm ready to get home. I never thought I would consider my apartment home, but ever since Junior and I have been hanging out—cooking together, eating together, and watching tv together—it feels more homey than ever. I don't know what I'm going to do when the lease is up and he moves on. It hasn't even crossed my mind that I may need to interview for a new roommate real soon.

I turn the music down so we can talk a bit.

"How did you like my parents?" I ask him.

He looks over to me and smiles, "I like them a lot. Your mom wants me to come back. I think she likes me," he tells me, laughing.

I laugh along with him. "She does, and so does my father. Thanks for offering to come with me. I had a really good time," I admit.

"Me too. I almost didn't want to leave. I'm a little

bummed out that I have to share you with everyone now."

I laugh. "Oh, so you want me handcuffed and chained to you, huh? Won't you get sick of me?"

He smirks. "I wouldn't mind you being handcuffed. Boy, the things I could do to you!" he adds.

I just roll my eyes. "Okay, I think it's time for some music." I guess that was the wrong metaphor to use. Guys get so easily distracted; their minds are quick to turn to sex. I turn up the music, and we chill in a comfortable silence.

A couple more hours go by, and I take over for awhile until we reach our last big stretch and switch again.

I open my eyes to look at the clock, and it's been about three hours since Junior took over. I didn't even realize I had dozed off. I guess my body was tired from all of last night's shenanigans. I yawn wide and long, and then stretch like a cat. It feels so damn good. I needed that nap.

"How was your little nap?" Junior asks.

I finish rubbing my neck. "My neck's a little sore, but I feel refreshed. I guess you wore me out a bit last night. Do you want me to drive?" I ask him. His butt has to be numb by now.

"No, we're almost home," he tells me. Looks like we've made it out of Pennsylvania, and we're now near Rochester. I'm excited to get out of this car. On the way down, I was enjoying the scenery, but now I'm just interested in getting back home and settled in.

Junior doesn't say much else; he looks to be in thought. I watch him as he watches the road. I almost don't want to know what's going on in that sexy head of his, but my curiosity wins.

"Whatcha thinking about?" I ask him.

He takes a moment before he answers. "I'm thinking about you, about us."

"Oh yeah? Are you thinking about us last night?" I question, trying to keep things light.

"Kinsey, what do you see for us in your future?" he says, laying a bomb on me.

I really don't know how to answer this. I feel like I've told him a million and one times what I want and what we are, but he still insists on asking me. It's honestly getting pretty annoying.

"I see us being friends, like we are now. Or at least until you find someone else, then we'll have to redraw the lines again," I answer, the best way I know how.

"So, you would be okay if I went out and found somebody else?"

"Well, yeah. I mean, if that's what you really wanted to do, then warn me beforehand."

He takes this in for a moment. "What if I meet her tomorrow at the grocery store unexpectedly? Would you be okay with that?"

My eyebrows furrow together. "I don't know, Junior. I couldn't tell you until that scenario happens. What is your deal anyways? We've talked about this numerous times!" I'm now beginning to get frustrated.

"My deal is that I care for you deeply, and I want you to admit to yourself that you feel the same way!" he says, raising his voice a notch. "I want you to tell me that you want to be with me just as much as I want to be with you! I want you to stop being so damn afraid, because that's not the Kinsey I know. You're unbelievably strong, stubborn, and you're not the same girl who got hurt back in high school. *I* would never hurt you, Kins! You and I belong together!" he finishes, banging on his steering wheel.

I feel as though all the walls of this car are closing in on me. I almost want to jump from this moving car just to get away from this all. It's just too much. He's going to make me lose it! "Junior, just *stop*, will you? You're asking too much from me. I'm not freaking ready for this shit! *Yes,* I care for you too. And *yes*, I love being with you just as much as you love being with me, but I'm not ready to think any further, Junior. I just don't want to get hurt," I say to him.

He smirks proudly from the small confession he was able to yank out of me. "Kinsey, I love every bone in your body, every hair on your skin, and every psychotic thought in that head of yours. I am undeniably in love with you. I can't help it; I fucking love the shit out of you!" he confesses.

My heart drops. I am completely speechless at this moment. Did I really just hear this come out of his mouth?

And then he drops another bomb on me. "I know you better than you know yourself. I know you have love for me as well in that heart of yours. I just wish you could admit it to yourself. Tell me something, Kins—"

I turn my neck toward Junior, and my life suddenly flashes before me in slow motion. This is it. My heart is about to skip its last beat and I'm about to breathe my last breath. We're going to die.

The air gets sucked from my chest as I try to scream out to Junior, warning him to look out. But it's too late. Two headlights come straight at his driver's side door head-on. Tires screech as he whips his arm out across my chest for my protection, and my head whips forward from the brakes. The scraping of metal bending and glass shattering is the last thing I hear before the lights go out.

A constant beep echoes through my head. I hear voices and strange sounds surrounding me in the distance. My head is piercing with a sharp, stinging pain. I'm in so much pain. I try to open my eyes. I will them to open, but they're too heavy. Please make this pain go away. I'm just so tired.

"Kinsey, can you hear me? Please come back to us. You're still needed here. We all need you. *I* need you. Junior needs you," says a small voice far in the distance. Is that Maxine?

I don't understand. Where am I? God, my head hurts. I hear that wretched beeping noise again. What the fuck is that awful sound? I feel a teardrop on my hand. It feels warm and tickles as it glides down my finger. I wiggle my finger to wipe it away and try to lift my eyelids, but they're just so heavy. I have to keep trying.

"Nurse! Nurse! Kyle, go get the nurse, she just wiggled her finger! Oh God, Kins! Please open your eyes. It's Maxine! I'm here—just please open your eyes!" she begs. I try once more with all my might.

Finally, I see some light through my blurry vision. I try to focus, but my head feels as though it's splitting in two. I close my eyes again to stop the pain.

"That's right, Kins. Open your eyes. You're doing it!" she says. A couple of other voices flood the room. I feel cold fingers on me, and I hear a voice I don't recognize.

"Kinsey, can you hear me? If you can hear me, just squeeze my finger," the female voice says. Is this chick crazy? I can barely open my damn eyes. I concentrate and move my finger. "Good, girl. That's it!" she encourages.

Who is this woman? I open my eyes again despite the pain. My vision is still blurry, but I see a young woman in front of me dressed in ... scrubs? Is she in scrubs? I don't understand. Where am I? Can somebody please stop this fucking pain? I open my mouth to speak, but I can't because there's a tube lodged in my throat.

"It's ok, honey. That's just a feeding tube. Don't try to talk right now. Is your mouth dry?" she asks while checking me over.

I nod slightly. "I'll grab a water sponge to swab the inside of your mouth. It will help with the dryness," she tells me.

I look around until my eyes land on Maxine and Kyle. Max is sobbing into Kyle's chest. Where's Junior?

Why don't I see Junior?

    I lift my hand up and see an IV stuck in my right hand. I turn my head slightly and then wince, trying to turn again toward that horrible beeping sound. It's a machine hooked up to the wires that now stick on my chest. I have only a gown on. Where is my underwear?

    "I'm going to give you some more meds for the pain in just a moment," the nurse says. A doctor comes in beside her and also begins his exam. I look to Max, wanting to speak, but this damn tube is in the way.

    "She's wants to speak. Can someone please get her some water?" Max asks.

    "She can't have any yet. We need to access her swallowing abilities first," the nurse explains. "She may have a hard time speaking for a bit. So it's better if you ask her yes and no questions so she can nod her head instead.

    Max grabs my hand. "It's okay, Kins Just relax. Everything is going to be okay," she tells me. I look around for Junior, but I don't see him. Where could he be? Why isn't he here with me?

    Max wipes the tears that run down my cheeks. The

door opens, and I see my parents rushing in. My mom is in hysterics as she runs to my side. Max holds her and assures her I'm going to be okay. I wince at the pain in my head. It's debilitating. I've never felt anything like it.

I'm so confused. I hear the nurse take my mother aside and mumble something to her and my father, but I can't hear over that beeping noise. I'm tired. I close my eyes. I just need to rest. I just need the pain to go away.

I crack my eyes open. The pain isn't as bad as before. I look down, and I see my mom plopped over my bed with her hand in mine, sleeping. My father is in the corner chair nodding off, and the lights are dim. It must be nighttime. I don't see Max or Kyle. I squeeze my mother's hand, and she immediately lifts her head.

"Hey, honey," she says to me before calling to my father.

I try to speak, but it's just not happening. The nurse is right. My mother brings a cup with ice chips to me and gives me a small piece. The cold wetness feels amazing against my throat, bringing life back to me.

I clear my throat. It's sore from the feeding tube and the dryness. My mother gives me a white board and marker to write with. "Where am I? Where's Junior?" I write. This is a difficult task, my muscles are so weak.

I see sadness take over her face. My heart drops. "Kinsey, honey, you and Junior were in a terrible accident. A drunk driver hit the driver's side door head-on," she says, breaking the news.

Tears begin to gush down my cheeks as quick flashes begin to come back to me. Oh God! Please don't tell me he's dead. Please, Lord! I feel as though my insides have been gutted and my heart's been ripped away from me.

I begin writing on the white board again. "Where's Junior? Please tell me he is okay!" I write in panic. This is frustrating. My hands can't keep up with my brain. She looks down for a split second, almost as if she's afraid to say it. I begin shaking my head as the tears continue to stream down my contorted face. It's probably a good thing I can't speak right now, because I would probably be screaming.

My father grabs my other hand to calm me. "Kins, Junior is still in a coma," my father tells me.

This means he's still alive; he still has a chance. "Is he going to be okay?" I write again since they never answered me the first time.

"We don't know, honey," my mother answers truthfully.

"How long have I been here?" I write. It takes me a moment to get my hands on the same page as my brain.

"Two weeks," my father answers. I begin to sob. Two weeks I have missed out of my life. I look down at my legs. My left one is in a cast; I immediately try to wiggle both my toes. They move, and I let out a sigh of relief.

"You broke your femur." My father says. "You were lucky you didn't break anything else."

"How bad is he?" I write.

"He has a lot of swelling in the brain. They can't tell if there will be any damage or not, so they have him in a drug-induced coma to help him heal so the swelling will go down. He has four broken ribs, a broken leg, and broken arm. His spleen was punctured, so they removed it, and his nose was broken," my father informs me.

I'm in shock. How could this happen to us? I need to see him. I wipe off the board with my hand. "Can I see him?" I add.

My mother squeezes my hand. "Soon, baby. But first we need to get you healed. They need to do another MRI to make sure there's no further damage to your head and to be certain all of the swelling has gone down. You've had a couple of them already. Kins, your head slammed against the passenger window as the car flipped over twice. You were both lucky you weren't killed," my mother informs me. I'm on information overload. I can't even process this all.

The doctor and nurse come in. My father sits back down in his chair to give them room as they check me over. They remove the feeding tube from me, telling me to exhale first. I gag uncontrollably. My mother's phone rings. She lets go of my hand and walks to the far side of the room so she can speak more privately. I wonder who she's talking to.

The doctor asks me some yes and no questions that I'm guessing he has to ask every head trauma patient; they're stupid but necessary, I suppose. My head begins to throb from all this interaction, so the nurse gives me some pain meds so I can rest. I close my eyes as they begin to kick in, and I fall into a nice, deep sleep.

I hear people talking around me. I see Max and Elise on either side of my bed when I open my eyes. They see me stir and stop talking.

Max grabs my hand. "Hey, Kins. How are you feeling?"

"Ice?" I ask with my raspy voice. I can finally speak a bit. She grabs my cup and hands me a piece of ice. Elise squeezes my hand and stands up to give me a light hug.

"I'm so glad you're okay!" Elise tells me. "We were all so worried about you."

I remember Junior and try to sit up more. My head aches as I move too fast.

"Kins, be careful. You can't just sit right up. You need to take it easy," Max scolds me.

I grab my white board. "How's Junior? Have you been in to see him?" I write.

They both look devastated. "Yes, we've all been taking turns between you and him, so someone is always with one of you. Kins, we won't know anything until his swelling goes down. He could recover fully or he could not. The doctors are doing everything they can for him. Did you have your MRI yet?" Max asks.

It's just like Max to tell it like it is. I clearly have rubbed off on her. I nod my head. Then I try to speak. "I need to see him for myself. He needs to hear my voice," I practically beg, barely getting the sentence out.

"I think that's a great idea, Kins, but maybe you should wait until after they get your results. You really should just be resting now," Elise tells me. I know she's right, but I just have to see him. He needs to feel my presence. I don't want him to give up.

"How are his parents holding up?" I ask, voice raspy.

"Connie refuses to leave his side, and Greg has buried himself in office work. Everyone was devastated when they heard. We let them know you were awake and healing," Max tells me.

I look across the room and realize it's covered in flowers and get well cards. I hadn't noticed this before. "Wow, look at all these flowers—" I whisper in shock.

"Yeah, everyone loves you, Kins. We were so afraid when we got the phone call. Kyle is a complete mess. I'm just glad he got a chance to make up and reconnect with Junior before this all happened," Elise says.

Anger and disbelief hit me. I can't believe that just came out of her mouth. I want to scream, but I can't. I just don't have the strength yet, so instead I write on the white board. "Don't say that! He's going to recover! He's going to be okay!" She reads it and looks mortified, because I've never been upset with her.

Her mouth hangs open like she wants to apologize, but nothing comes out. I begin sobbing like a little baby. Max immediately rushes to me and holds me. "Kins, honey, that's not what Elise meant at all. She's just saying that for

Kyle's sake or else he would be beating himself up even more right now," Max explains, trying to calm me. The more I cry, the more my head throbs. I just need to see him.

"Kinsey, I'm so sorry!" Elise apologizes. "I didn't mean to upset you."

I feel like a horrible person for getting angry with sweet Elise who wouldn't hurt a fly. I reach my hand out to her, and she comes to my side to embrace me. We all stay this way for a while until Jeff comes to get Elise. They stay a while longer, then they head off to visit with Junior after my parents show up.

A couple hours later, the doctor returns and give us the good news that my injuries are healing well, and there is no more swelling in my head. They will be moving me out of ICU and down a floor. I should be able to be released within a couple of days.

Once I get situated in my new room, I ask if my mother can wheel me down to Junior's room, and the nurse agrees.

I get off the elevator and cruise down the hallway. Junior's room is located one floor up from mine. There's constant movement between the staff and doctors, and visitors coming and going. My heart pounds against my chest as I worry about how he may look. Will I be able to recognize him? Will he be able to hear my voice? My heart is a wreck right now.

We reach his room, and my mother slowly wheels me in. Connie, Junior's mom, is sitting beside his bed. She looks over to me and begins to sniffle as my mom wheels me closer. Junior is lying on the other side of her. I still can't see him yet. I hear the heart monitors beeping and the ventilator machine pumping his oxygen for him, because he can't breathe on his own. Tears begin to slide down my cheeks. I feel the air being sucked from my lungs. I don't know if I can really do this now.

Connie comes up to me and wraps her arms around me while crying on my shoulder. I almost feel as though I need to be strong for her instead of the other way around. It is her son lying in bed, still in a coma.

"Kinsey, dear, are you sure you are up for this?" Connie questions before moving out of my way. I gulp loudly and nod. She moves to the side of my wheelchair, and there he is, full of wires and IVs. He looks so fragile and helpless as the machine pumps his lungs full of air. I do my best to hold back my tears. I have to be strong for him. I can't break down. He needs me.

My mother wheels me over so I am now sitting next to his bed.

"We'll be right outside," she advises me. I nod my head, because I don't have the strength to speak yet. I grab his limp hand with both of my hands and bring it up to my lips. He feels lifeless. I'm so used to him squeezing back. I kiss his hand gently and hold it up to my cheek. I sit just like this for a while, watching his chest pump up and down until I can find the courage to speak.

"Junior, it's me. Can you hear me? I've been thinking about the last question you were going to ask me before this all happened. You asked me to tell you something—but you never got the chance to finish. I want you to open your eyes and ask me. I know you can hear me. I remember bits and pieces from being under. I heard noises and voices, but they were so far away that I couldn't get to them. I couldn't find my voice, but I fought, and I made it back.

"Junior, you have to fight. If not for yourself, then fight for me, fight for us. God, I was so fucking stubborn, and I was so scared. What if you realized you didn't want me? I can be erratically crazy at times, but what if you decided you couldn't handle it anymore—then what? I would crumble into a million pieces if the man I loved decided to walk away.

"I wasn't ready to accept the risk. I wasn't ready to take that chance, but I am now. If anything, this accident has taught me that today is all we have, and tomorrow isn't promised. You asked me to jump with you; well, I'm ready. I just need you to take my hand, Junior. I need you to wake up so we can spend every minute of the rest of our lives together. I love you. Please come back to me. Please—"

I can't hold it in any longer. My lungs constrict and burn, because the air can't get through. I'm hyperventilating; I feel as though I've been stabbed in the heart over and over again, and its being ripped apart piece by piece. It's taken all this time to realize that I love him and that I was in denial. I've loved him all along. I just refused to allow myself to see it. It's taken this accident to happen for me to open my eyes. It takes everything I have not to scream from the top of my lungs. I feel like I'm dying inside as I watch him, appearing lifeless and covered with wires and surrounded by machines.

Connie and my mother come rushing in as I fall apart. I can't stop crying. I'm gasping for air, and I can't calm down long enough to take a breath. "Kins, just breathe. It's okay, just breathe," my mom whispers, trying to coach me. I can't lose him before even getting the chance to tell him. That's all he wanted to hear, but I was too chicken to say it—and now look.

My head is throbbing. I feel as though I might pass out. My eyes roll to the back of my head and sweat begins to bead around my forehead as the pain becomes unbearable. My vision fades in and out, and I can't tell if it's from the pain in my head or the pain in my heart, I just need to rest. "Nurse! I need somebody in here!" Connie runs out of the room, screaming for help.

I had a panic attack when I was visiting with Junior. My blood pressure shot up, but they put me on medicine to regulate it. Visiting him for the first time was intense, but now I know what to expect. It doesn't make it any easier, but I'm handling it a bit better now.

It's been three weeks since I've been home without Junior. My apartment feels downright depressing. I haven't laid a finger on my bed. I've spent every night sleeping in Junior's room, blanketed in his smell and our memories. When I'm not sleeping, I'm with him at the hospital.

His bruises are beginning to lighten from his broken nose. Once the swelling began to go down around his brain, they took him out of his medically induced coma. They won't know the extent of any long-term damages until he wakes up and they can assess him. It's been a little less than two weeks since then, and he still has not woken up yet. The doctors say he is in a vegetative state, which means he is present but doesn't have the ability to interact with his environment.

His doctors still have hope, and I would never give

up. My mom's been great. She closed her shop for the time being so she could stay with me and help. I will have this cast on for at least another week or so. It's a pain in the ass to get around, but I'm managing with the crutches.

My head injury is still healing, and I have moments of quick, severe pain. I've been getting migraines often, but the doctors advised me this is normal for the next six to twelve months. The nurses get upset when I stay in the hospital too long, because they know I need my rest. But they also understand being here is important for my healing as well.

Yes, I look like a hot mess. I have bags under my eyes, and I've probably lost a good ten to fifteen pounds. But I don't give a shit about myself right now. Connie comes in after work to stay with Junior and forces me to head home. She won't take no for an answer.

The girls have been amazing. They do what they can and show up unannounced so I am forced to socialize and get some girl time in. I was ignoring everyone's calls when I was released from the hospital. I fell into a major depression, cried while curled up watching Lifetime movies, and the girls refused to allow me to take pity on myself. They were right; I was alive and doing well and Junior needed me.

The elevator door dings open to the intensive care unit. The nurses and doctors are roaring in full effect. This place is like Vegas; it never stops or rests. I greet all the nurses I have come to know by first name as I head over to Junior's room.

It's Saturday, late morning, and Kyle has fallen asleep with his head back and mouth open in the chair next to his brother. I rub Kyle's shoulder to wake him. He stirs awake and looks around. "Oh hey, Kins. I didn't even mean to fall asleep. Penelope was up all night; she's teething. I'm exhausted. I probably shouldn't have come up here, but I just had to see him," Kyle tells me.

"Has anything changed?" I asked.

His face goes cold. "No, no change. My mother said the doctor mentioned to her last night about putting him into a private care facility if he doesn't wake up anytime soon or get any better. She would have called you, but she knows you need your rest."

"She should have called me regardless. I don't understand, is this protocol?"

He shrugs his shoulders and grabs his jacket. "I'm not too sure," he answers before looking at me. "Hey, Kins, how are you doing with all this?"

I put on a front. "I'm doing as best as I can like we all are. I'm not giving up. I refuse to give up."

He nods and then rubs my shoulders. "My mom will be up in a couple of hours," he tells me before leaving.

I open the blinds and refill the water in a vase of flowers. I kiss Junior on the cheek and then pull up the chair next to him. I put his hand in mine, rubbing it against my face.

I tell him about my morning and how my mother is beginning to drive me insane for the first time in my life. I tell him how hard it is to get around on these damn crutches and that my armpits are killing me. I know if he can hear me, he would be shaking his head and laughing at me as well. I just wish I could hear his voice. I take a deep breath and relax, just sit with him in complete silence, praying to the man above to bring the love of my life back to me.

A tear slides down my left cheek as I kiss his hand.

I scooch up in my chair, careful not to mess with his wires, and I lay my head lightly on his chest to listen to his heart beating. He's fighting in there; I know he is. There's no way he would leave me. He's my world, and there's no world without him.

I try to nuzzle into him, smelling him, but he doesn't smell like himself. I wish he would just open his eyes, because I feel as though he is slipping away. "Come back to me, Junior," I whisper. "Please come back to me."

I stay this way for what seems like hours. I only get up to use the restroom. When I re-enter from a bathroom break, Junior's eyes are open. I freeze, blink, and rub my eyes to make sure I'm not seeing things. Is my mind playing tricks on me? Am I dreaming?

I slowly walk over to the bed, and he turns his head to look at me. I take in a breath and cover my mouth. He's awake! He's really awake! I immediately reach over and pound on the nurse's call button on the side of his bed. Then I gently pick up his hand and squeeze. He squeezes me back.

"Oh my God, Junior. I can't believe you're awake!" I say ecstatically, tears gushing down my face. But before I can tell him I love him or lean down to kiss him, the nurse walks in. She takes one look at him and calls for more staff.

I back away so she can do her job. Another nurse and doctor come rushing in. His eyes remain locked on mine the whole time. A low fire burns within as his eyes blaze into mine. I feel the connection, and I can feel our love flooding the room. I'm immersed with power and completely encompassed with devotion.

I swear in this moment, between the man above and I, to love this man with all I have for the rest of my existence. I release my breath; I know everything is going to be okay. *We* are going to be okay.

EPILOGUE

Junior

"Are you ready, bro?" Jeff asks with a silly smile.

"I'm ready as I'll ever be! I've been waiting for this moment ever since I set my eyes on her," Kyle tells us. He still looks nervous as hell.

"You're a lucky man, little brother," I say, patting him on the back. "Don't mess this up! You already know Kins will come after you!" I tell him, laughing.

Kyle whistles and nods. "You ain't lying about that!"

This whole moment is surreal. We are inside the MGM Grand in Las Vegas. I am standing next to my brother and Jeff while waiting for our girls to descend down the aisle. My little brother is finally marrying the love of his life.

If you asked me a year ago if I would be standing next to my brother at the alter, I would have said hell no! But since then, I was also fighting for my life, and he was there by my side. I was in a coma for over a month. It was the strangest thing. It was like being in a mucky haze—almost dream-like. I heard voices and saw shadows surfacing from time to time, but no matter how hard I tried, I wasn't able to communicate.

I have very clear thoughts of this one particular moment—I remember there being excruciating pain, the type of pain that one can never comprehend until they experience it, and then there was a flash of light and my pain was gone. A sea of light had opened up in front of me. There was nothing but pure, beautiful, warm light. It made my mind free and my soul calm. Such an unbelievably serene moment. I walked toward it without a thought or consideration of possible danger. It was as though danger didn't exist. Everything that light exuded was full of peace and beauty, something that just felt so right, until I heard her.

I heard her voice, and I could feel her tears on my

skin. And then I heard it. Those three simple words. It was so clear and so truthfully pure that every inch of my being came to life. A rush of blood started pumping furiously through me, pounding in my chest and hammering through my ears. If I walked through the sea of light, my heart would be left behind. It wasn't my time. I turned back toward her voice, and my choice was made.

The moment I opened my eyes and saw her, I knew I was where I was supposed to be. It has taken me months to get back to where I am now. I still get nightmares since the accident, but Kinsey loves me, and that's all that matters. Everything else is just a hurdle I will overcome, because she is by my side.

I watch Elise walk down the aisle, and she looks absolutely beautiful. I look over at Jeff, and he has tears in his eyes. It's kind of a magical thing to witness. Who would have ever thought that Jeff, whose life was only about partying and girls growing up, would fall in love?

I look back toward the aisle, and there she is. Time freezes and my heart swells as Kinsey walks toward me in her beautiful bridesmaid dress. I see now why Jeff teared up. I've never seen anything more beautiful and perfectly perfect as I do now. This woman has marked me, tattooed herself onto my heart and engrained herself into my soul. Every breath I take is because of her.

She mouths those three powerful words, "I love you," before she takes her spot next to Elise. Her love is what allowed me the choice between life and death. Her love is what keeps me going every single day. She's my everything. My world means nothing without her.

The change of music drags me from my thoughts as Maxine glides down the aisle with Penelope holding one of her hands and Luke guiding her other. My throat tightens up as I watch this scene unfold. My mother sniffles from the sidelines, and my father looks proud.

Penelope lets go of her mother, and her tiny hands reach out as she heads down the aisle toward Kyle. She has a gigantic, bright smile on her face. We all laugh as he scoops her up and gives her kisses, and all I can picture is the same for my future.

The nuptuals are filled with brilliant tearjerkers, and we all whistle and clap as the reverend announces them as husband and wife. Tonight has been a magical night full of family, friends, and unconditional love.

Kinsey and I drift off, heading to our room. I kick off my shoes, take off my jacket, and loosen my tie. I pour myself a drink and follow her out onto the balcony. She looks so peaceful, searching out onto the luminous lights of the strip. It's now one in the morning, and the street is still live.

I lean against the balcony next to her, watching and studying her, thinking how lucky of a man I am to have her. She looks over at me with a seductive smile. It's her classic Kinsey smile I know so well.

I run the back of my fingers over her cheek, and she leans into me, closing her eyes. She is irrevocably tantalizing. She opens her eyes to look at me. "I love you, Junior," she whispers.

I lean in to kiss her. "I love you too, Kins," I reply. I can't hold my desire and longing in any longer, so I blurt it out. "Marry me. Just you, me, and God above as our witness. I want to be tied to you in every way possible. I promise to love you until my last breath. Just please say yes." I hold my breath as I wait for her to speak.

She has tears welling up. She nods her head furiously before saying another word. "Yes! Yes! I will marry you, Junior!" She then jumps into my arms.

I laugh out loud, wrap my arms around her, and swing her around the balcony, absolutely thrilled. "We can go now, right down on the strip to a little chapel!" I suggest, holding my breath and waiting for her answer.

She thinks for a moment. "You mean now?"

I nod. "Yes, now."

"What about about your parents and mine? What about Max and Kyle? And Jeff and Elise?" she asks, beginning to panic.

I grab her face between my hands and stare at her intensely. "Kins, we nearly lost our lives. We escaped death! But somehow we survived. Not by chance, but by God's grace and our love for one another," I release her and take a step back with my hand out to her. "Take this leap with me, Kins?"

She bites her bottom lip, looking down at my hand. She then looks back up to me and smiles. She puts her hand in mine. "Okay, Junior. You jump, I jump."

THE END

About the Author

Shevaun DeLucia, author of the *Eternal Mixture* series and *A Forbidden Romance* series, lives in upstate New York with her husband, four children, and two dogs. As a stay-at-home mom while her children were young, she fell in love with reading. She indulged in the small moments that took her away from the reality of her loud, rambunctious household, bringing her into a world of fantasy. When reading wasn't enough to satisfy her, she turned to writing, determined to create the perfect ending of her own.

Social Media Links

Website: http://shevaundelucia.com/

Blog: http://shevaundelucia.com/

Facebook: https://www.facebook.com/pages/Author-Shevaun-Delucia/563843076961083

Twitter: https://twitter.com/shevaundelucia1 | @shevaundelucia1

Goodreads: https://www.goodreads.com/author/show/7375844.Shevaun_Delucia

Amazon Author Page: http://www.amazon.com/SHEVAUN-DELUCIA/e/B00U9YB33A?ref_=pe_1724030_132998060

Newsletter: http://shevaundelucia.com/newsletter/

IG: https://www.instagram.com/author_shevaun_delucia/

Google+: https://plus.google.com/u/0/118067787943597283181/posts

TSU: http://www.tsu.co/AuthorShevaunDelucia

Acknowledgments

I cannot believe this is the last book of the *Forbidden Romance* series! It feels so surreal, and I have many to thank! First and foremost, I want to thank my editor, Jinelle Shengulette! She has been with me from day one and continues to polish my work into beautiful, readable novels! Thank you for all your hard work and late nights!

To Dana Hamm and David Santa Lucia, my cover models—you brought my vision to life, and I couldn't be happier with the result! You both are amazing inside and out. I feel blessed to have worked with you on this project, and I'm excited about more to come! And to Scott Schisler, *Nirvana*'s cover photographer, thank you for the amazingly perfect cover picture! Your talent in capturing the perfect photo and your eye for beauty is such a gift! I Can't wait to release the others to the world!

I also would like to thank my cover designer, Sommer Stein, for the hot, sexy, and gorgeous cover you created! And to Amy Donnelly for formatting *Nirvana*— I'm excited to work with you both in the future!

And big thank you to my incredible, hardworking PR team, The Next step PR! Vicci, Amber, Helena, and Sybil: you are all truly awesome, and I am so thankful to have you all by my side. And I have to give a special thanks to Kiki and Ruth—my mentors, my backbone, my friends—thank you for being my personal cheerleaders and pushing me to my limit! I don't know what I would do without you all!

Thank you to my friends and family for all your encouraging words and support!!!

Last but not least—I can't forget my readers! Without you, none of this would be possible! So thank you will all of my heart! You rock!